TIMECLOT

Titles by D.D. Cross

Timeclot

Chrome Plated Corns

Me and Mr. Mephistopheles

Onions Bunions Corns and Dungeons

A Den of Brigands

Field of Corns

Forheavenstake

Back to Hades: Eustice Seeney Returns to Hell

Go to Hell! (I DID): Interview with Eustice Seeney

Devilzinthedetails

Hellitainteasy

Heapatrouble

TIMECLOT

D.D. Cross

MMA
Publishing

This is a work of fiction. Names, characters, places, and incidents are the products of the author's imagination, or are used fictionally. Any resemblance to actual events, locales, or persons, living or dead, is entirely coincidental.

 Published by the MMA Publishing Group International.

ISBN-13: 978-0692314685

ISBN-10: 0692314687

Original Art by D.D. Cross

Manufactured in the United States of America

“Life has become immeasurably better since I have been forced to stop taking it seriously.”~Hunter S. Thompson

“If you're going to kick authority in the teeth you might as well use both feet.”~Keith Richards

“The people trying to make this world worse never take a day off.”~Bob Marley

“We are what we pretend to be, so we must be careful about what we pretend to be.”~Kurt Vonnegut

“If time travel is possible where are the tourists from the future?”~Stephen Hawking

FIANCHETTO: The development of a bishop by moving it one square to a long diagonal of the board in the game of chess.

PREFACE

September 13, 1970

Operation Tailwind was a covert incursion into southeastern Laos by a company-sized element of U.S. Special Forces, and Montagnard Commando Hatchet Force of the Military Assistance Command Vietnam Studies and Observations Group (MACV-SOG or SOG). Military Assistance Command conducted between September 11, through September 13, 1970, during the Vietnam Conflict. The purpose of the operation was to create a diversion for a Royal Lao Army offensive, and to exert pressure on the occupation forces of the People's Army of Vietnam (PAVN). A US F-4 Phantom encountered mechanical issues and released ordinance resulting in the destruction of a

South Vietnamese hotel. The fighter jet returned to base intact, and the incident was declared accidental. There were no reported casualties.

TODAY

A STRANGE VACATION

Linda Boznak leaned across the front seat spilling chips on her husband Lem's lap."Lem look at that!"

"What is there a cop behind us?" Lem slowed down.

"Did that strip mall go up overnight?"

"Honey I'm drivin' here, who cares about another shopping center. Shit, you got corn chips all over me and the seat," he said frantically brushing off the crumbs. "Dammit they'll get in my pants and my nuts'll be all crusty."

"You and your stupid privates."Linda said.

He shoved her aside, brushed off the superficial chips, and dug his hand in his pants. The nineteen ninety-eight Buick station wagon drifted into another lane, the wrong lane. It took a broadside hit by an eighteen-wheeler sending them spinning.

Linda's bag exploded with the windshield spraying confetti into the car's interior, along with a squall of glass, partially hydrogenated impregnated corn chips, shards of cornstalk, road dust, and debris on impact.

Her mouth froze in an "O" as she was just about to holler at her husband of thirty years, that his balls have been crusty for twenty-eight of those years. The Buick rolled once and skidded onto the roadside, disappearing from the highway into the oblivion of a cornfield.

The truck's driver knew the cops would chalk it up as another roadside calamity. The big rig's true owner, Elmo Kumberbach, would tell the highway patrol his truck was stolen from a rest stop earlier that day. The authorities didn't buy Elmo's story that it disappeared while he was emptying his bladder. Especially when the paint matched up and the truck's contents were revealed. The soon to be abandoned vehicle would turn up with sufficient evidence to change Elmo's life trajectory forever. The hit-and-run driver would be far away counting the money for this little caper. He tooted the horn as he accelerated.

Lem couldn't be sure how much time passed as he came to, suspended upside down by his seatbelt. His ears hurt and were still ringing like someone took a sledgehammer to the soundboard of a baby grand. He just hung there until his wits returned to him.

His first thoughts were provoked by the crumbs that fell out from his waistband and hit him on the chin. So much for ball crust, then he saw blood. Linda was out and not wearing a seatbelt, she might have broken eight bones to Sunday. Judging by the crimson on her white muumuu she was dead, dying, or close to it? He felt okay, the airbag did its job. Too bad the passenger side didn't have one. Linda was a mess. Did he feel that bad about her being a little bruised and unconscious? At least she's not talking. Oh well. He undid his seatbelt and gathered up his rag doll hemorrhaging spouse. This was going to be a mess.

At least she wasn't dead, or was she? Check the pulse, yep that'll do. Her head didn't flop back so her neck's not broke. She didn't piss or shit herself. Yeah, she's breathing. Hmm, the life insurance is paid-up could just leave her, that'd be easy enough. Nah, too many questions and not many answers. They'd been fighting in public too. Not worth the hassle with retirement a few months away. What if she goes into a coma and needs round the clock care? Shit. That could screw things up. Not going to just leave her are you? Guilt creeping in isn't it? Yeah. Damn wishy washy as always. Lem you bastard can't make a decision if your life depended on it. He ran a hand through her heavily lacquered hair. He considered leaving her for the paramedics as an option. Yeah, that might work. He grabbed a few stray chips and chewed them while waiting for a siren. Which after ten minutes, the appropriate time to wait, didn't.

Finally Lem lifted Linda and cradled her. He thought it better not to unstrap her bag. Damn women and their purses, hang on to them like their lives depended on `em, and began walking. He looked at the damage to his car as they walked away from the wreck toward the highway. Maybe he missed it, but there was a shopping center across the highway. Damn, he'd been dazed from the broadside blast, maybe he just wasn't thinking clearly, but another strip mall? Eh, what else is new in this stinking country. Every two miles a drug store or grocer. So Lem and his unconscious bride-cradled in his arms-began hiking toward the strip mall. Bitch was heavy as shit. Where are the cops when you need `em? How much farther is that mall anyway?

Why would anyone in their right mind build a shopping center in the middle of nowhere. There must be a doctor in there. Maybe a walk-in clinic, some quack couldn't cut in regular practice. Worse comes to worse there's got to be a dentist.

Linda and Lem Boznak were on their annual cross country vacation. They delighted in the same trip from Golden Springs, Florida, to Cleveland, Ohio, every summer. To take in the scenery and enjoy the delightful rest areas where they'd pull in, park, piss, and spend the night.

Across the United States strip malls pop up in locations once considered isolated, remote, or just plain senseless. Why put a chain grocery store in the middle of nowhere? Nobody really gave much thought to how many strip malls there were until there were so many of them. The land couldn't sprout a thing but more broken glass, asphalt, and puddles of oil.

As far a strip malls go, they're an innovation to maximize real estate in confined areas. In America everyone's selling something. Strip malls need an "anchor store," which often if not always is a branch of a well financed, heavily invested-either privately or publicly owned, grocery store or pharmacy.

Grocery stores worked well because they take up the most square footage, pay the land owner and or investors the most rent, employ plenty of folks, and pay plenty of taxes. Power companies benefit, shippers and handlers of everything from soup to nuts, cows to beer, and everything in between sit on shelves, frozen food sections, or bakeries at grocery stores.

Fruit pickers in distant lands toil for pennies, so locals in flyover state USA can earn minimum wage, cheap health insurance, and a retirement plan. John or Jane Doe ham and egger can retire in one of those distant lands where the fruit, vegetable, or coffee beans grow, and not starve to death. Then again it looks good on paper. In some communities the mom and pop town shops are put out of business by the big outlet stores. Is there public outcry? Sure, but it doesn't last long. At least not long enough to piss off customers who used to pay ten bucks for the same bullshit they could get at the mega-chain market for pennies on the dollar. Add a pharmacy tag on free prescription drugs—not all, just the cheapest—and you've got an oasis in a wheat or corn field.

The outlet store at the mall Lem carried his wife to was called Giant Yummies. It was smack dab in the center of the strip mall, next to the Chinese takeout, Lucky's Laundromat, and adjacent to May-Li's Vietnamese nail salon. There was a chiropractor, a podiatrist, Tarot reader and medium, dentist, and an outlet shoe store to boot. Lem had plenty of choices and shit she wasn't exactly a bag of feathers. From Lem's standpoint on the road he could make out a glimmer. The setting sun must've caught some broken glass or something, and it sparkled, tickling the light like Koi Fish in a clear pond. Somebody was there.

2

WATCH OUT FOR STRANGERS AT STRIP MALLS

The parking lot of the strip mall had a grocery store at its axis. The hub of rural America looked bustling from a distance, but the closer he got to it the setting sun revealed a nearly empty parking lot, almost abandoned. There was only one car parked in the lot, and a man smoking a cigarette leaned up against it. The unmistakable tail fins of the red Cadillac convertible—in Lem's mind—were the “classic” car its owner knew it to be.

The man next to the Caddy wore a black leather motorcycle jacket over a pair of jeans, that from a distance looked filthy. However, upon inspection were not filthy at all rather very high end, along with the shoes, wristwatch, and some sort of electronic device he was fiddling with. The man had Elvis style hair, mutton chop sideburns, and aviator sunglasses, he was looking at his watch when he heard Lem holler out.

"Hey buddy, little help here?"

Caddy man ignored him, opened his car door, and sat down behind the wheel.

"Hey buddy, I got a sick person here."

The Cadillac driver started the engine and revved it. A plume of blue smoke filled the backside of the vehicle. Maybe this fucker'd get the hint and beat it, if he knows what's good for him. He flicked his cigarette out onto the asphalt, and fiddled with the settings on his radio. Finally he settled on something with a distinctive beat loud enough to discourage the old geezer carrying the broad from coming closer. Can't have that. Not now, not here. Just beat it old man. He pushed his shades up his nose, tapped them, and stared straight ahead.

"Hey buddy I'm talkin' to you." Lem was ten feet from the Cadillac, and from that distance he could see the man's wristwatch. It was late afternoon and he could make out the face of the man's timepiece.

Must've been where the glare came from—it was some kind of mirror. What the . . . "Hey buddy," Lem thought the guy either was ignoring him or was deaf, but he couldn't be deaf if there was music playing. Shit this bitch is heavy. What's with this leather jacket dickhead?

He didn't even turn his head in their general direction, or rev the engine, the car just idled with music wafting into the open air.

Odd sounds too, Lem would recall. He couldn't place it right then but knew it was from a movie, an old one. If he would have recognized the movie from which the song was part of he may have had a hint about this guy's story.

The nail salon's door flew open and a woman ran out. She looked like she robbed the place. Wearing a straw hat and black silk pajamas she ran like the dickens right to the back seat of the red Cadillac. She got in and shouted something before they sped off. Skinny little thing—oriental? Shit what's going on here? Lem watched the driver shout back at her over the seat, point at her, and set into jabbing his finger at her like she was a bad dog. The driver slammed the door. Boom Boom Boom someone ran out after them, and he had a gun! Shit a fucking pistol, fired it three times at the tail end of the car as it sped off.

Lem was lost. “Where the fuck is this place? Am I in Ocala, Orlando, Ohio, or Oklahoma? His arms weakened and Linda Boznak suddenly weighed more than he could handle. It felt like gravity ratcheted up a few notches and his eyelids got heavy. Lem knelt, and lay his wife of all those years down on the parking lot over the tire tracks of the car with the freaks in it. “Assholes” he muttered, watching the cars tail lights. Just embers in the distance surrounded by nothing but fields and fields of wheat, corn, and barley. Where were the stinking cattle? He began to sob when out of nowhere he heard a voice.

“Burt Winn, buddy I'm Burt Winn, and you look like y'all need a bit of help palso.” He said tucking the pistol into his waistband. “Bit-a-help, that's what I'm here for. Win with Winn they say around these parts. Put `er there palso,” he held out his hand. “I'm the man with the plan around these parts, let's get the little lady a look see.”

Lem held up a hand and wiped the moisture from his face with his shirt sleeve. He cradled his wife with the other. “Winn. 'Win with Winn,” he rolled the words around in his mind. An urge to vomit welled up. He tried to spit but his mouth was too dry. “I got to get her to a hospital. I can't fuss around. Are you gonna help?”

“You betcha palso, you betcha. Lemme help yah out. Looks like you can use an extra set of arms . . . Uh, I didn't git yer name palso.”

“Lem. Lem Boznak from—”

“The Lem Boznak?”

“Hey my wife is bleeding asshole. Are you going to jerk me around or act like that other asshole that drove off without even a stinking nod.”

“Hey palso hold your horses, I'm—”

“Jerking me around. Now help me get her to the clinic over there dammit.” Lem lifted her limp body, jiggled her a bit to try awakening her. Nothing. Is this asshole going to do anything but blab?

“Hang on, the clinic's closed.” Winn said, taking a step back. “I'm allergic to blood.”

“What do you mean the clinic's closed? Where is everyone?”

Winn glanced right, left, then tilted his head toward Lem and Linda. “I got to tell you Palso this ain’t the right time for this you see.”

“No, I don't see anything but a creep. Now get out of my way. I'm taking her to that nail parlor that freak ran out of. Maybe they can call an ambulance.” He broke off the conversation, and started walking toward the salon.

“You don't want to do that.”

“Get out of my way.”

At that Burt Winn removed the pistol from his waist band and aimed it at Lem's forehead. “I can't let you go in there palso.” He hit him dead center in the head. “You're not gonna be rememberin' a whole lot Lem, are you?” He kicked him in the ribs.

3

2014 Florida at the Oasis

Daphne Frellen was celebrating her twenty-eighth birthday at The Rosemary Garden, with her on again off again, somewhat imprecise, as her mother would describe him, boyfriend. Assad El Khouri, the fourth cousin to the former Emirs of Bukhara. The nation state existed from 1785–1920 when it fell into the hands of the Bolsheviks. It is now within the boundaries of Uzbekistan. An often touchy topic upon Assad, also known as "Chip," for the purpose of awkward random police stops, airport screenings, and general principles alone.

Chip was equipped. Tonight he'd pop the question, and soon Daphne would be swept from all this to his lair in the Kingdom in Dubai, where he retained the title "His Excellency Prince Assad El

Khouri in Exile." A notable man of means whose family fortune: twelve camels, six palm trees, and an oasis—forty six, by fifteen square feet lay over millions of barrels of oil per day divided per mathematical equations yet determined. Allowing such generous hospitality to the young El Khouri and his current four wives and sixteen children.

Daphne, rarely considered herself anything but a fine Christian woman and recent graduate in art history with aspirations in philanthropic acquisitions and estate dispositions. A most beneficent patron of the arts would indeed find this pleasant red blooded American articulate, precise, and knowledgable. However, this was certainly in direct opposition to that of her parents, who considered her for lack of kinder terms: "A whore."

Nonetheless, when she did consider herself she was often showered with gifts from the on again off again boyfriend. Whose latest gift a late model Mercedes Benz coupe brought them to this fine five star eatery housed with pride of purpose on the prized beachfront property in Palm Beach, Florida.

"Daphne," Chip said, while draping his napkin on his lap. "I hope you are very pleased with your new automobile, no?"

“Hold on Chip, my phone's buzzing—” She dug her long polished left hand into the Chanel bag. Another gift months beyond the latest style, for her smartphone. She held a finger to her lips, faked a pout, and turned to look at the phone to check out who was calling.

Chip raised an arm to motion the sommelier to the table. He'd already refused the waiter's offer for drinks with a firm:“It is against my religion.” Most fine restaurants maintained the service for high end guests, especially those who'd meticulously detailed their plans earlier. Something suggested to Chip there'd be a slight change in plans, and perhaps some social lubricant for this situation might be in order. The server prepared in advance, courtesy of a clandestinely slipped C note by Chip upon their arrival, stood next the table, bowed slightly, and patted his palms on his thighs like he was about to take off. “This is Gene, our wine expert,” and held out an open palm in his general direction. “He's an expert in all types of—”

“Bring the best the very best Champagne.” Chip flashed his eyes at his blonde American woman chatting quietly on the phone. She was nervously twiddling the Tiffany's necklace that tickled her décolletage. “Daphne” he said, do you have any—” She cut him off with a shooing hand.

“Just bring the very best. One glass. One glass for the lady” Chip said, and stared at his date's impressive chest mounds. Certainly refreshing topography after a week in Qatar. An oasis lie between those luscious melons. Yes, yes. No expense spared for this treasure. But these Western ways? Ah, for now, it is not so much distraction as the pleasure in studying how this silly nation and its silly ways cherish such silly things. Chip took a deep breath, reached for a warm roll, and comforted himself in knowing this restaurant would soon be part of the sea, and Daphne would be very far from this disgusting world. Pigs.

4

1958 HOOGERSTOWN USA

At the corner of Main and First Street in Hoogerstown, the Beaufort Building stood with pride of purpose overlooking the town's major intersection. There hadn't been much traffic since the expressway was built by the Army Corps of Engineers. They left off the exit ramp to the town as most highways built in the United States were done as a function of moving troops, supplies, and ordinance, quickly and efficiently to one port or another. Hoogerstown had no value.

According to officials in the Pentagon this rural town had no strategic use, and was deemed such in all searchable databases. In effect the signing of House Appropriations Committee findings pretty much wiped Hoogerstown off any map with respect to any practical purposes. However, there were purposes, some extremely impractical, which had gone unseen by any and all decision makers holding elected office.

Failure to capture what was once a heavily trafficked route, the interstate became the bane to its existence. Passerby traffic for practical purposes of the town's citizenry was for some devastating. Outlets for farmers selling portions of their harvest ceased, and the mom and pop restaurants and shops failed to thrive.

Despite the town's isolation a curious investor would find this just fine for a new project. An island in a sea of acres of farmland. The townspeople were elated when the mysterious investor infused life into the sagging economy. Apple pies were selling at the diner again, the movie theater was showing the latest films, and the bar was packed nearly every day with townspeople and the off-kilter people who worked at the new plant.

There was an unspoken rule amongst Hooger's folk not to say boo to the "new" people. They were busy buying lumber and building materials from local vendors, shopping at local grocery stores, and eliminating the cobwebs. Facilities that shriveled up like the old day drinkers at Nick's Bar. Occasionally they would stumble out into the mid-day sun and catch sight of an architectural oddity that always struck a chord in a person's psyche.

Nick's Bar is across the street from the Beaufort Building. It is wedged between a shoe store of the same name: Nick's Newest Shoes, and Tina's Nail Emporium, Nick Pontini's cousin.

Two doors down is Nick and Lou's the town's only authentic Italian restaurant. Despite rumors, Nick and his cousin Lou, the bartender at Nick's Bar, grinned when customers inquired about the restaurant as if it was like, you know "connected." They'd reply with a wink. The black and white newspaper clippings of famous hoodlums, photos of Frank Sinatra signed: "Loved the food Nick and Lou," by none other than one of the cousins. The "mobbed up" milieu was one they worked hard to maintain. Neither were in any way "connected" to organized crime.

However the notion they "might be" gangsters was good for business, and kept folks from trying to skip out on a bill, complain too much about undercooked veal, or watered down wine. The Pontini clan originally moved from "back East," in the 1930s, and maintained the impression that Al Capone might show up one day and order lasagna.

No structure was taller than the stone and marble building across the street that was the centerpiece of the town. Its first floor housed the town's sole furniture store, and what in later years might pass for a department store, butcher shop, and tailor. Between the ten cent store and pharmacy was a double glass door with a directory listing the professionals occupying the floors above.

The single elevator next to the stairway in the lobby of the Beaufort Building had an "out of order" sign taped to it. If asked, the buildings super Clark Gully, a man not quite particularly inclined to answer questions, would refer you to the management company, who made arrangements with Clark by mail, to maintain his residence in one among many storage rooms in the building's basement. With strict instructions to keep the floors swept, lights on, and the lavatories clean and functional. Simple job no responsibilities outside the world that made up a collection of professional offices, and wouldn't recall just how long it had been out of order, simply that.

On the second floor of the building was a dimly lit hallway of offices, with brass plates on the doors. It smelled cloyingly sweet like a dentist or doctor's office. Scrubbed down and wholesomely clean—maybe too clean—that made something about the place seem to an astute visitor like a movie set. Once your eyes adjusted to the light, a person could feel the air was a little off, almost as if gravity paused, but that sensation wouldn't last because the piped in music had a certain rhythm that was interspersed with the burring of a dentist's drill, or was it. By the time you decided it was maybe just part of the music you'd already be late for your appointment.

Doc Beaufort's General Practice office had a single door with an ornate doorknob, and seemed to be on a hinge that shut behind you just so. Upon entering you'd swear you knew you were in the waiting room. You might not hear the singsong chime indicating you arrived as the door swung shut. The icy whoosh of air that sent a shiver down to your bones.

“Hello, can I help you?” A woman's voice came from across the room. Before you know it the door behind you makes a barely audible whirring sound, like tumblers falling into place and a bolt seals the door. An ordinary Jane or John Doe might be surprised, but for CP and Grinder, this trip from 2014 to 1958 was just business as usual.

5

BACK TO 1958

"You found the girl in once piece, good." The woman in the peaked nurse's cap said in a voice so soothing Grinder considered having his prostate examined.

"Shut the fuck up Grinder," CP said. "I know it looks like the 1950s but I can still read minds, and this Milly is—"

"Li." Smokin' little number at that. "Miss Li is just who Beaufort wanted to see." Grinder said.

"May-Li, Grinder, her name is May-Li, and Grinder your prostate's fine." Milly said.

“All right, all right. I can give her a quick physical if you'd like. Kinda get her ready for Doc B.” Grinder was using a handkerchief he'd taken from his pocket to wipe his hands. “No problem.”

“Shut the fuck up Grinder, you're not tubing this woman.” CP shook his head. “No totally unnecessary breast exams for you today joker. Didn't that get your license suspended for a few months? Put away the snot rag.”

“One month CP. Just that, and they knew it was a bogus claim. That exam WAS necessary.”

“Grinder you're truly unbelievable.”

He ran a hand through his hair, and patted his mutton chops. “That's what they say.”

“Sure they do Grinder, you douche bag.” CP said. “Now just sit down and wait.”

6

BACK AT THE RESTAURANT

Daphne put the phone back in her bag and smiled at Chip. “So how was your flight?”

“I ordered some Champagne.”

“I wanted a vodka tonic.” She crossed her arms under her breasts. “I really like ordering for myself Chip.”

“I was only thinking of you, my sweet little flower.”

“Sweet little flower? Come on Chip you can do better than that,” she said shaking her head and biting down on her lower lip. What a schmuck. At least he delivered on the car. A few strands of hair fell across her face caging it, so her bright eyes seemed to peer out like green lanterns.

Chip leaned forward and reached across the table brushing aside her stray hairs. She slapped his hand down.

“What are you doing?” She quickly pulled back the stray hairs and tucked them behind her ears just as the server set an ice bucket next to her. “Oh,” she said counting the calories in her mind. Drinking a full bottle would add up, and require exercise to work it off. That's what it would take to get her loaded enough to deal with Chip. The awkward disrobing, and five minutes of penetration before Chip's final thrust. Asshole.

7

BACK AT THE PARKING LOT IN FLYOVER LAND

Burt Winn had himself a “situation.” What to do what do do.

“Are you gonna shoot us or help us out, 'palso'?” Lem delivered a knee to Burt Winn's crotch at full throttle sending him gasping, dropping him to the parking lot. The gun spun around twice and came to a stop. Lem snatched it up and aimed it at Burt's crotch.

He hefted up his bleeding wife, making adjustments for the shifts in movement. “Let's get moving 'Winner' Winn, what say you?”

“You betcha palso,” Burt said offhandedly. “You betcha.”

8

NEW TRUTHS FOR EDDY

"Truth? Shit. I must have lived in a vacuum isolated from reality. It seems like the decade slipped by without realizing just how shitty the US economy had been. Now I know it was just a trick. A trick to enslave us, all of us stupid Americans wasn't it?"

"Edward, Edward, Edward, please clarify. What you're saying might be indicative of what we look back as. Sort of population control." Beaufort said. "Your perspective is from a person who came of age in another era. Maybe putting your views in perspective—" Doc Beaufort appeared out of thin air. "Tell me about what you've been doing Eddy."

"Here, let me clarify this: I was walking along the dock and ran into a guy, and we got to talking. We were rapping about some bikini clad, wine sipping ho, on the fantail of some big mother of a boat. The name 'Time Flier' stood out like a cleft palate when I saw it was titled out of the Cayman Islands. I knew somebody's stashin' something, somewhere, and made a note to check it out."

"I know who it belongs to Eddy, don't bother."

"I walked over to the parking lot with the guy and saw his car. I asked if he minded telling me how much? Forty-five thousand bucks. Holy shit? 45K for this piece of shit-I didn't mean to say it out loud. Lie number two: "Nice ride man. I walked on thinking to myself: what happened? What's the value of money?"

"Well, well, well Edward, you're looking into things that may put you in a rather nasty situation. I suggest you stay to yourself."

"What am I doing here Beaufort?" Eddy asked.

"In time Edward. In due time all the pieces will find their way into the right puzzle."

"The hell's that supposed to mean?"

I thought back to what forty-five thousand bucks bought in 1984. Shee-yatt, I bought a fine Mercedes Benz rag top. It was not only superbly made it was reliable.

“This is the way of civilization, emerging technologies, and valuations.” Beaufort said.

“That same car goes for a buck twenty-five today. The same shit-just more gizmos. I don't think I need it to make me a safer driver. I think all the onboard computers are just things to fuck up, so you can take cars into mechanics trained in Silicon Valley’s latest greatest dashboard tech, right? The value of 1984 dollars bought more “stuff, and a C note was, well it was worth a hundred bucks. That's not the way things ARE is it?”

“In 2014 dollars, a hundred bucks is worth about fifty cents. So anyone that suggests there's no inflation is pretty much full of shit. I noticed the gradual ratcheting up of prices of little things, coffee, wine, etc., that stuff crept up on account of increasing oil prices, and those two hoodlums 'Shipping and Handling.'”

“Interesting.” Beaufort said.

"Can you please give a little hint about what I'm doing here or why? This place is making me nuts."

"Well, well, well Edward, I'll share this, you certainly know a bit about the biggest underground, above ground, ongoing criminal enterprise that Shappelino and Handberg started way back in a secret meeting in 1928 with Henry Ford, Thomas Edison, Flagler, and Al Capone, to perpetuate for years to fund the secret 'Check Engine Light' society."

"Grinder mentioned that to me, the 'CEL Society'—Yeah."

Beaufort pushed away the air with a broad sweep of his hand. "We'll skip that for now. What's relevant about the early part of the 21st Century with respect to the value of money is—"

"What are you sayin'?"

"Well, well, well," He held up his palm. "It had been a form of population control and social engineering. The most salient feature was the great 'Affordable Care' laws. Hilarious, yet an ingenious enslavement of the US."

“Yeah real funny Beaufort. Some healthcare reform.”

“It certainly was emphasized to those watching the value of currency, wasn’t it?” Beaufort said.

“I don't see it that way.” Eddy dragged a palm across his face.

“The value of money was lowered, and folks weren't ready to face the fact that a five thousand dollar deductible isn't that big of a deal in the grand scheme of things is it? It's a rationing of sorts. The price of things went up, but the amount of money earned by Joe and Jane ham and egger has not. It hasn't matched the dynamic of keeping up with the decades long decline in value, and that's what's vexing. So there's a healthcare system which is remarkably fouled up, 'value' in its paying 1980’s dollars for 2014 items, services, and of course training. In a broader sense the economy's rate of inflation had gone up, up, up, but incomes remain stuck in another era—1980s dollars. I don't know if this is making sense, but I can't imagine how a person could support a household on 70-125K, raise kids, send `em to school, and just “survive” in any comfort.”

“Maybe.” Eddy said.

“Use simple arithmetic Edward. Go on—”

“If you do the math and have a 200K student loan debt—an iffy potential—to hop on the hamster wheel, you're just going to stay afloat.”

“Yes Edward, things had gotten quite odd.”

“A doctor, once had some “certainty” regarding a place in society where they'd be assured a decent living. Those concerns are overshadowed by all the forces encroaching on them: Extenders being salaried for more 21st Century dollars beyond medical doctors. Dentists hustling to do the latest greatest with equipment that costs more than a 2014 Bentley X3. Essentially the middle of America's society gets wiped out.”

“Criminal activity grew in so many ways.” Beaufort said.

“There's a wasteland that's gone unchecked, largely ignored, and with the Kardashians, NSA spying, and the kid with the hoody’s trial, misdirected America's been doing something else while the stock market climbed, but not the mid section. This healthcare law, as it unfolds, is going to get plenty of non-participating millennial's who'll be buying molly, and getting tattoos and piercings. There's some funky shit going on, and I don't know what it is. But truth, the thing we're supposed to be 'now seeing' seems pretty far off."

"Did you notice anything else Edward?"

"Yeah, the boat was registered out of a place I couldn't figure out because it was written in Chinese."

"Edward, Edward, Eddy my good man, THAT is exactly how currencies were manipulated to maintain the development of the first time portals. Nobody had the time in America to look beyond their own lives. Anyone who did got little, if any media attention, books published or read, and we controlled the public domain–anything–in the public domain."

"Misdirection."

"Yes Edward. What the eyes see, the ears hear, and appetites crave, the mind believes, and desires."

"It was all done right under our noses wasn't it?"

“Oh, we did have help, didn't we?” Beaufort said. As Milly, Grinder, Nadine, and—”

“Emily?” Eddy remembered her from . . . he couldn't recall. “Beaufort I'm losin' it help me out here?”

“Well, well, well, given a trigger a vague recollection becomes a fuller recollection. Emily was with the Time Bureau. For a spell we sent you back to the 1800s. You spent some how shall I say this, ah, 'quality time' with her before bringing you to this era. She's gone now.”

“Yeah, I do remember her, and some hick in a pickup truck who took me through some—”

“Portal, Edward. The man in the pickup truck does some work for us from time to time.”

“Will I ever see them again? Either one of them?”

“I doubt if you'll see the woman. However, you never know when you might need a ride Edward. You just never know.”

“That's just great. What have I gotten into here Beaufort? Tell me.” Eddy turned his back to Doc Beaufort and began tapping his foot.

“In due time Edward in due time.”

Eddy turned to look at Doc Beaufort and he was gone. “Shit, now what?”

9

INSIDE THE SALON

The Laundromat next door to the May-Li's Nail salon had several cushy chairs with trays beside them. There were two chairs raised above the others with little foot baths next to them. These were what Lem imagined to be specially designed chairs because they had little trays that slid out at the foot section. Upon inspection, the inscription from the manufacturer said: “Detritus Tray” which the nail workers used to collect nails pieces and corn and callus shavings.

Lem placed his wife in one of the plush chairs, her purse strapped over her shoulder, and stepped back. What a relief. Shit. He was taking in the abandoned and silent salon. He was just turning to face Linda when the door swung open.

"What's that?" She said.

"Burt, I don't want any trouble from you. Not anymore. Do you get it?" She pointed the pistol at him. "Now step back."

"No Lem you step back." Linda had a small pistol in her very steady hand, and cupped its grip in her palm. Burt taught her well.

"Want me to hand over my pistol?" Burt took three steps toward Lem. "Winner Winn, they call me, looks like I win palso."

"What exactly do you think you've won winner?" Lem said, just as his wife shot him.

"What did you have to do that for?" Burt said. "Minga dinga. I can't believe you didn't wait till we were in the alley. Shit my ears are ringing, and there's blood splattered all over me. Minga dinga."

"How do you think I feel with this shit all over me?" She said lowering the pistol, and began dabbing off the blood. "That was disgusting."

"Sweet cheeks it's going to work out just fine. Don't you worry your pretty soon-to-be twenty-one again head."

"You do know what you're doing Burt, right?" She closed her mouth, and twitched her closed lips from side to side. "I just killed my husband." The corners of her lips turned down.

"Sweetie, how many times do we need to go over this." He placed a finger on her lips. "Turn the frown upside down, the clown had it coming anyway and you know it."

"You were supposed to do that." She quipped.

"Prick kicked me in the nuts dammit."

"And took your gun too Mr. Winner Winn, swell work."

"He's the one that was screwing your sister, remember that?"

"Let's just get things taken care of before—" He looked over his shoulder. "Is that a siren in the distance?"

“It sure sounds that way doesn't it?” Linda got out of the chair and started sifting through the detritus tray. “Come on Winner, we've got to get this down, and get out of here.”

“I'll drag him over to the cash register and make it look like a robbery.”

“Burt there's no one here to rob. Maybe you didn't notice but Li'-May’s not exactly here?”

“Shit. Just hurry up. We don't even belong in this decade.”

10

DOC BEAUFORT

The man behind the desk had on a white coat over a Glen Plaid vest, part of a bespoke suit. There was a chain across the vest's buttons the patients could see as he leaned back. The chair squeaked but it broke the droning sound of the air conditioning, and the hum from the X-ray view box.

"Nice lungs." Grinder pushed his sunglasses up his nose, gave a tap between his eyes, and dabbed his hands on his hair before reaching into his leather biker jacket for his cigarettes.

"Don't smoke in here Grinder," the man next to him said.

"That's fine CP," the Doc said.

“She's a much more powerful spirit than I'd thought guys.” CP said.

“Well, well, well, not one to mince words CP. What makes you say that?”

“He's full of shit Beauf, she didn't say 'boo' in transit?”

“Did you just say 'boo' Grinder? Shut the fuck up. You drove like a fucking maniac till we got to the vortex.”

The man behind the desk raised a hand, “portal CP, portal. Only one available to this spot. A direct tear in the fabric of time that opens up right—”

“I know I know, outside this friggin' pissant town in nineteen fifty, in the middle of a cornfield.”

“What is it about shutting the fuck up you don't understand Grinder?” CP slapped his palms on his thighs. She didn't speak at all. It was as if she knew what we were doing, why we nabbed her, and where she was going.

“So's I could keep an eye on her.” Grinder flipped an ash on the floor.

“Here, use this.” Beaufort slid a coffee mug across his desk. “She is, from what I saw of her quite self-aware.”

“That's not good, is it?” CP rubbed his thighs.

“You got an itch CP? I think you dig Miss China Li, eh? Nice perky little tits.”

“Asshole, she's a fucking machine.” CP reached to his right where Grinder leisurely smoked and rocked in his chair and smacked him in the back of his overly primped coiffure.

“Hey,” the front of Grinder's chair hit the ground with a whoosh. “Shouldn't there been a thump? Shit, the wood floor—”

“Grinder you're in another dimension. My dimension,” Beaufort said. “Newtonian physics do not apply here. You know that, CP knows that, yet you can not get it through that self-indulgent mind that you are here for a reason. Snap to it Grinder. Snap to it or you might just find yourself passing through another porthole into a punitive point in time not so amenable to your particular personality quirks.”

“Who you callin' quirked Beaufort, huh? I didn't ask for this shit. I'm a friggin' doctor dammit, not some bounce about roughneck on bullshit errands.”

“Yes we are Grinder.” CP said. “I'd like to go back to my cozy pad too.”

“Yeah that smoking' babe in 2070 eh?” Grinder said it out loud.

“Now now now boys let's cooperate and piece together May-Li's oddly placed nail salon throughout the Twenty First Century, shall we? Oh CP, Nadine's here with Milly and in the process of dissecting the most efficiently designed android.”

“She still has some nice tits.”

“Shut the fuck up Grinder.” CP and Doc Beaufort thought, then spoke the words in unison.

Grinder pulled the coffee mug from the desk, held it up, and dropped his cigarette into it. “Then riddle me this Batman, how the frig does a robot send off vibes like that? They've got no functional amygdala, pituitary, adrenals, or hypothalamus? The rapid conversions that set off pheromone conversions aren't mechanized, machines can't metabolize. She's got to be—"

"Some permutation of human." CP said. "There's more Grinder, I didn't say anything but I dozed during the ride. I dreamt and then May-Li got in."

"You dug those knockers too, eh CP?"

"She spoke to me in my dream."

"Go on." Beaufort leaned slightly toward CP.

"She didn't use words, no, she was more of a presence pressing against my thoughts."

"Shit, there's no way friggin' bots can dream jump. Didn't that get outed from the design of all machines in the beginning?"

"Yes it did. The automatons remained cerebrally incapable of any semblance to thought processes beyond their programming." Beaufort raised his hands. "Now remember the idiots who wanted to store their consciousness in their computers in the early Twenty First Century? All the rage. Live forever kooks, way before the C-phone wars, and Mymine chips not even a dream. Strict consciousness storage via computer. An utter failure."

"I remember those jokers," CP said. "Didn't work, all they could store was memories. A bunch of cognitive relays amounting to nada. Sure they could reflexively make cute party gags, but they never 'lived on' in the form of computer app. Total bullshit, and nice scam too. Plenty of suckers bought into that. Didn't you get in on that hustle Grinder?"

"Hey CP, ain't funny, man."

"With the advent of nanotechnologically driven additional cyclic nucleotides, as you two know all too well, having our DNA laced with orbiters programmed and reprogrammed with each breath, each moment is impossible to mechanize. A uniquely human innovation unless—"

"Unless someone somehow figured how to develop human cells sans preprogrammed cell death-apoptosis."

"And they didn't shed, or get dead," Grinder added.

“Oh dear.” Beaufort said. “The rungs of the DNA ladder of May-Li may very well transcribe, translate, and thus hack into the satellites. She's an integrated evolutionarily designed automaton, capable of cellular regeneration, reproductive anomalies, and to any extent history's known . . . Human.”

“Who would do this? Why would they do it Doc?” Grinder shrugged and tapped another cigarette out. “Wouldn't that fuck up the,” Grinder held up both hands to make parentheses with his fingers, a cigarette dangling from his lower lip, “the natural order of things?”

CP looked at him and shook his head. “Shit, Grinder you're not as dumb as I thought you were.”

“No CP he's remarkable dumber. Amygdala?” Beaufort said stroking his chin.

“Now what?” CP notched his head.

“Well, well, well.” Doc Beaufort took a pocket watch out and flipped it open. “That's simple boys we stop them before they begin.”

“Hang on a second,” Grinder stood up. “I didn't sign on for jumping in and out of time again.”

“Yes you did asshole. Now sit down or those smokes WILL kill you. You want to go back to your moron era? I sure's hell don't want to live life without what I’ve got now.”

“That's correct boys, once you've been converted you're converted for life. However long that is.”

“Easy for you Beaufort, what're you six hundred years old.”

The door burst open just then and May-Li had an arm around Milly's neck, a scalpel to her throat. “Nobody move Yankee Doodles.”

“Hang on cupcake let's talk about this,” Grinder said.

“Shut the fuck up Grinder,” CP murmured.

“Okay dokey Yankee Doodle with rocky roll hair gimme key, and you come with me. You drive.” She said pointing her chin at Grinder, pressing the scalpel's blade hard against Milly's neck.”

“Grinder she's taken the blood we drew from Nadine and injected it into herself. Do as she says, do it now or she might—”

“Grinder don't be a dick, go.” CP stood, shifting his weight from his right to left foot he said to Li “If you've harmed a hair on her fucking head you're a dead fucking robot bitch.”

“You funny CP real funny I already dead. Come now Yankee Doodle looky you friend say you come with me.”

“Go with her Grinder.” Beaufort said in a soothing tone. He scanned the room pausing a beat, to the other folks in the room he spoke as if he was delivering a dire diagnosis: “I want you all to understand that this entity can hear and understand our thoughts, so do not think she cannot estimate your considerations to action.” He locked eyes with Grinder. “Do as she wishes and make sure Milly is unharmed. Does everyone understand?”

Grinder stood there, an unlit cigarette hung from his lower lip. “You gotta be kiddin' me.”

“Grinder, don't be an asshole, do it.” CP said.

Within minutes they heard the Cadillac's engine rev, tires burning rubber on the street. By then Beaufort and CP were in the exam room with Nadine. She was laying on the floor an empty syringe dangled from her antecubital fossa.

11

VIEW FROM NICK'S BAR

Nick was mopping the mahogany bar when one of the day drinker's held up his beer mug for another round, and casually glanced out the bar's window. He'd seen the Cadillac convertible parked there earlier and admired it, but now looking beyond the beer mugs couldn't figure out what the hell was going on.

"Hey Lou whaddya doin' I need a refill. Are you in space or'd a Sputnik land on Main Street?"

"Shut up Poop. What's going on over there?"

Poop was Hoogerstown's notable drunkard, poet, philosopher. Often found rambling mostly to himself at Nick and Lou's at any given hour, on any given day. "The hell you talkin' `bout Lou?"

"The hell they doin' over there? Two dames and a beatnick?" Lou said tossing the bar rag onto the wood plank.

Poop's barstool squeaked as he turned toward the window. "Whass goin' on?"

"Looks like that skinny broad in black PJ's got some kinda knife up against Doc Beaufort nurse's neck."

"Yeah. How do you like that?" He held the mug up. "About that beer."

"Hang on Poop." Lou reached under the bar and came up with a baseball bat. Louisville Slugger. "Accept no substitutes when some heads need bustin'. Poop, hang on a second I gotta check this out." Lou ran toward the bar's entrance.

"I'm comin' Lou I'm comin,'" Poop dismounted the barstool lost his footing and stumbled out onto the street to join Lou Pontini who was slapping the ball bat's sweet spot against his palm as they both watched the red car speed off.

"That son of a gun crashed a red light." Poop slurred.

"Something fishy's going on here." Lou considered how involved he wanted to get in this imbroglio.

He liked that word, and wondered if getting involved in it might be bad for business. A little attention might not hurt and decided to call on the sheriff.

"How about that beer Lou?"

"How about a whiskey too, Poop."

He handed the drunkard the ball bat. "Put this away I got business to take care of. Just don't finish the bottle and pass out on the floor."

"Where you goin' to?" Poop watched Lou walk toward the corner.

"Business Poop, taking care of business. You go mind the store and don't touch the cash register. You know I'll know."

"I don't steal nothin' Lou, I don't do nothin' like that."

The words were lost on Lou Pontini who was deliberating how he'd frame the situation of the "kidnapping of the Doc's nurse" to tell Sheriff McGroosky.

12

IN GRINDER'S RAGTOP

I never wanted any of this shit. Life was good for me, and now this? Shit. Grinder lit his cigarette and inhaled deeply. “Where we goin' cupcake?” He said.

“Just drive Yankee Doodle, just drive till I say.”

“Do it Grinder,” Milly said. “Now you can let go of me May-Li.”

“I asky you lady? You shut face or I cut you good I cut you real good ruin Mr. Rocky Roll car real good.”

“Hey now cupcake, those are—”

The two women were in the back seat of the Caddy where May-Li held one arm around Milly's waist, the other curled around her neck, and the scalpel's business end still pressed against her right carotid artery.

“Just do as she says Grinder, and don't hit any bumps.”

“I no to happy on you Milly you try kill May-Li. Not nice lady. Make chop chop look for DNA. No no. I hold you real close lady. I hold you real close till I know you no get tricky tricky.”

“Cupcake,” Grinder slowed the car. “Stop being a friggin' bitch, you're being chauffeured by yours truly to wherever the fuck you want to go. You can lighten up on the Mekong Delta shit.”

“What you know from that Yankee Doodle, huh? You drive, you drive fast or I kill future lady—you hotsy totsy girlfriend?”

“How the fuck does this a nail salon ho know squat about squat?” he said. “I'm drivin' I'm drivin' okay? I want to listen to some music, you cool with that?”

"I dig plenty tunnels without no musical. Mr. Rocky Roll kill plenty Yankee Doodle like you. May-Li no kill you now maybe kill you later. You like May-Li now? Drive the stinking car."

"I'm drivin' I'm drivin."

"You do that Yankee Doodle. You drive too slow Makey faster I busy woman you know that, right?"

Grinder began thinking about another era, and said: "DARPA, do you know what that is?"

"Big hush hush secret US money money, spy toys."

"It's a little complicated May-Li. They might be watching us."

"Who care Yankee Doodle just drive. DARPA scmarmpa. They can look up my coolie hole find nothing."

"May-Li, it's the US Defense Advanced Research Projects Agency for creating and preventing strategic surprises. The DoD set it up after the Ruskies launched Sputnik in 1958, and cooked up the internet—as regular folks know it—along the way. Trillions they say, Freaking Zillions of dollars go into it. Every fucking thing from Huxley and Leary to Buck-freaking-Minster Fuller's been figured out by scientists."

"Okay, there's that. Why should I give piece of crap Mr. Rocky Roll?"

"You never know who's watching," Grinder said.

"Watch what Elvis? I just hard working immigrant."

"No, you're right May-Li. Whatever you say." Freaking broads. Always right. Just shut the fuck up and do what she wants. Broads.

"Just drive. Business to do, chop chop." She shooed her hand. "Just drive no more talky talk."

13

CURVE DOCTORS

“You know, I think it's the curve. People don't get it,” Grinder said.

“The fuck are you talking about Grinder?”

“Some people don't get it.”

“Get what?”

“Doctors who gotta really wrestle and fight to get to be doctors.”

“The fuck you talkin about. You go to college, med school ready, then boom, MD. Easy peasy.”

“Yeah, and those guys who ain't seen or lived the curve fuck up the most.”

“That's on account they don't know from the curve.”

“The fuck you sayin'?”

“Take Joe Schmo, he goes from Point A to Point B, college, med school, residency, boom boom boom. The closest point to B is to go the straight line, dig?”

“I don't know what you're saying.”

“Okay, you go from NY to Paris it ain't a straight line.”

“No, you gotta account for the curvature of the earth.”

“So the distance’s gotta be figured in right?”

“Yeah.”

“So guys who don't figure in 'the curve ain't got no sense of all the other shit goes into traveling from point A to point B.”

“Okay so if this doctor had to go learn Swahili and live in the jungle starting from point A would he —”

“He'd get to point B but look at all the shit he did in between.”

“Yeah yeah, he'd be fuller of information.”

“Yeah, he digs the curve, lived it, so he got something you're AB cat ain't got—”

“Yeah, curve guys.”

“Fuller? Shit, man you got some idiom issues and a fucking robot whore pumped up on stolen nanochips that we, my friend, need to figure out how to stop.”

14

THE GATHERING CORNS

Burt “Winner” Winn cussed out loud: “Corns and dumbass nail shavings. Shit, they contain DNA—big deal. I look like some kind of fool. Oh but that's exactly why they're here—why I'm here. A damn corn swiper. Shit. Look at those dumbass foot chairs, they stink like old socks, feet, and ass.” He continued scooping and cursing to himself. “This shit better be all they say it is. Shit, shit, shit on a stinking stick.”

“What's that sugar?” The widow Linda Boznak said.

“Nothing. Not a damn thing. Shit, these things look like cornflakes Burt honey. I wish May-Li was here.”

"Do you know what you're doing Burt? This is fabulous."

"Yup, just ducky. I know what I'm doing, go check the back door and I'll take that lump of shit—"

"My husband's a lump of shit. Real cute Burt."

"A dead piece of shit Linda. Now are you gonna get rolling or what?"

"Haven't you had enough of this shit?

She looked at Burt's corn collector bag and shook her head. "We need a little more, Burt."

"Baby, I got corns like you wouldn't believe."

"Let's hope we have enough."

15

WHAT TO DO WHAT TO DO?

CP said to Grinder, “If you dig a six foot hole you find a couple bodies, maybe three. But if you dig a nine foot hole you might find fifty.”

“Are you saying I should cool it?”

“I'm saying get another shovel, and start digging.”

“Someone's dug deep enough they've discovered that they can shift their lot in life, Grinder.”

“And we're supposed to stop them CP? That's not my friggin' job is it. Damn my feet hurt.” Grinder sat down and took off his zip up half boots, and began rubbing his feet. "Shit I could use a ho like May-Li givin' me a little rubba dubba, dig?"

"Grinder what's that thing in your shoe, a lift so you can look an inch taller?"

"Two inches dick head, as if I need to look any cooler than I do. Asshole, it's a friggin' arch support. An orthotic some douchebag chiropodist made for me. Protects my corns from getting worse. They give me balance. Dig?"

"Not really. You're better off going bare foot than using that shit to fuck up your balance. Especially if we're going to be on the move."

"No man, these things have scientifically been demonstrated to maintain smooth sailing anywhere you strut."

"Really, that sounds like bullshit."

"Let me explain something to you CP, these things," Grinder held up one of his shoe inserts. It was plastic, and shaped like the sole of his foot. "Custom made baby, custom made. You see, the foot is a loose bag of bones, when it makes heel strike and transitions into a rigid lever to propel the body from gravity's pull. Every step you take, hundreds, maybe thousands of times a day. The muscles, tendons and ligaments get orchestrated like a symphony just-so. Friggin' science man. Friggin' science."

"Seriously, Grinder, you buy into that bullshit?" CP picked up one of the shoe inserts and held it up to inspect. "You think this enhances diddly?"

"Shit yeah. The foot guy said it 'makes for a dynamic and fluid movement with each step. You know the basics: Our leg bones rotate, hips swivel, and vertebra align and realign with every step. A well fitting custom designed orthotic placed in your shoes can assure the most fluid transitioning from a bag of bones to rigid lever assuring a balance in the gait cycle. Besides, I didn't have to pay for `em, the quack who made these owed me."

"Grinder you dipshit. Fifty-thousand or so years ago man left the caves to hunt the plains for animal flesh barefoot. The foot's structure is such that shoes are unnatural attempts to redefine the body's natural function. The shifts and adjustments during the gait cycle trigger sensory organs within joints and ligaments sending signals through the spinal cord to the brain, which shuts off some muscle groups, and stimulates others. This delicate interplay among structures is a natural imperative for maintaining optimal muscle capabilities via local vasculature (constrictions and dilations of micro-vessels) defining the sort of fibers involved in the interplay."

"Go on, I forgot this stuff," Grinder said.

"The array of muscle groups transitioning alternate between fast and slow twitch fibers routing and rerouting oxygen demand, and enhancing cardiac output to satisfy mitochondrial function and the consequential electron transport necessary to sustain life. Any attempts to curtail this interplay will have a profound effect on cardiac function."

"I got friggin' cramps and spasms, along with the friggin' corns, CP."

"In effort to restrain the spastic contractions and release of muscle groups resultant accumulation of lactic acid alters the sodium potassium balance with heightened renal excretion and retention. Leading to an unwholesome condition for optimal function of the of the cardiac cycle. This can result in tachyarrhythmias in feet, stabilized by shit like this 'orthotic' device placed in human shoes, to restrain natural function really fucks you up. You're better off going barefoot."

"What're you sayin' CP, I should toss these things —for eight hundred bucks—and suffer with corns?"

"You're better off having another smoke than trying to fuck with the way you walk. Your muscles gotta work out the kinks on their own and adapt."

"So that gives me an idea. May-Li may have been shaving off corns and—"

"Setting up her own little scam? She's done it before, and came here to lay low."

At that, the world started to shift. The barometric pressure dropped, and the temperature changed by ten degrees. They looked at each other knowingly. Both men were aware something in the world shifted at some other time than the one they were in. The sky's color turned from day to night, and the world unwound.

Suddenly they were somewhere in the teen years of the twenty-first century. It began with the reformation, almost a punishment, of America's health care system. A political or some other bugaboo occurred somewhere that enabled a handful of magnificently profitable companies, pharmaceutical and insurance outfits, to take absolute control. Control of the nation's healthcare from cradle to grave. That was a long time till it happened though, as things stood in 1958.

"It's the chance of a lifetime Grinder."

"I don't know."

"You can't pass it by."

"Bullshit. I can do what ever the fuck I want."

"You aren't gonna be getting another chance Grinder," CP said.

"How do you know that?"

"I know. Believe me I know it. I've seen this shit before."

"Bullshit. Beaufort hipped you to—"

"Maybe he did Grinder. So what?"

"You fucked me over man. Why should I trust you?"

"Because buddy, I'm all you've got."

"Is that supposed to be comforting?"

16

BEAUFORT TELLS CP THE BEGINNINGS

Without preamble Doc Beaufort told CP history took a bend in the road. “It began years ago with DARPA. The Defense Advanced Research Projects Agency. Then there was the FDA Act of 1968, which modified regulations in such a manner that many of the 'approved' food additives were mind numbing. In many instances 'mind controlling' substances rarely if ever became known in the public domain. I'll get back to that later CP.”

“Tell me how this was viewed from 2070?” CP said.

“Well, the Defense Advanced Research Projects Agency (DARPA) had free rein over their special projects, and were accountable only to themselves.

There was a 'Cold War,' but even if there wasn't the USSR would have been some other unseen enemy to justify advances and discoveries for use on a battlefield, any battlefield. War has been part of humanity, and the US was going to be ready—no matter what it took."

17

CP ASKS HIMSELF: HOW DID I GET HERE?

As ordinary as any day could be, my feet even felt more same than same, which meant it couldn't be real to be some logically illogical malevolence. I couldn't put my finger on. But I can't feel my fingers because they're numb. What the—

Where am I? How did I get here? Everything looks the same but it isn't the same as it was. It never was and there's this tiring sense that things won't ever be the same as they ever were, or maybe I'm just getting older. Older and tired and can't see where I'm going and what's what. I don't know what's what. Where and what it this place? Is this a dream? How long will I be in a place where nothing is what it was? Am I dead? No, this has to be a dream, yes, a dream—or is it?

Nothing's making sense, and the cares don't show up, and my mind's empty and there's not a thought I can pull into it. My brain's stuck and there's not a word, a thought, an idea, that can ever flow into me. I'm in some midst of some mist like a cloud of crazy swooped down and drowned me, and I can't breathe—but I can, and take a deep breath.

Cool, cool, cool, that's the rule. Play it that way, show nothing. Close to the vest, keep it on the DL and never ever do diddly. Pop a Valium, wait, wait, wait for it to kick, and then stumble with those same feet that are cold. Colder than fucking hell and the rug—filthy mat of rotten fabric—is that reality? Is reality just a piece of carpeting? A stupid rug is the extent of the limits of my mind? I miss my dreams they were more real than reality—at least the one I'm in.

My skin's tight. Firm, flowing, moving, I can feel my muscles, tendons, and ligaments flowing under it. I can stand up. I feel it now, something oddly . . . but what's odd. I closed my eyes, and awoke into a dream that was a mish mash of monstrous pleasantries. Everyone there nudged me for this, that, or some other shit. But that's nudging.

Who was it in my dreamscape thats's always there. It comes in different forms. Whispers in my mind's ears. Colors, images, and sounds without audible context. There are no decibels in the quiet of night only railroad cars hitching up, trains on tracks in a distance so close that's nowhere but the place in my mind. Off world places not real, but more real than this. What is this? Where is this on a map but a place in my mind that's only truly tangible beneath my tongue. The taste in my mouth is bitter and my teeth hurt.

Piss and wait. Smile, floss, mirror me my own image. How old am I? Where did the years go? I'm in a place that's not a place, but it's cool, warm, safe, soft, and there's a hum of something-the sound of decency. I can see the atmosphere and it's a light blue hue, tinged with gray and shadow, and the sounds hiss on. Onto the next phase of my moments.

Does it get more difficult to wake up each day as years unfold. Do years really unfold? Is that some warped saying that means nothing, or some oddity that time does fold over onto itself like an accordion or series of events that go on over and over until they end? I feel crinkly, and today can rub shaving cream on my face and tough the skin. Sandpaper.

Salty and pepper flecks of bristle like some insect fucked my great grandmother and bugged her pregnant. Shit my gene pool's been cannonballed by some bug. Mother fucker. No not that. My father wasn't an insect and that grasshopper TV show on the Discovery channel with bugs fucking was pretty cool.

I spray shaving cream on the mirror and the room freezes. Shower's on. Steam's coming up wrapping around my eyes. I can't see. Another perk of years on earth. Things stop focusing into shape, need these special eye focusers. Why though? Why would we be built in such a way that the world we see naturally starts getting blurry? Why do we have to reach out to get shit to make the world come into focus that was easily seeable when younger? Hang on, I hear a color of someone's shirt in my dreamscape.

They didn't need glasses. Nobody wears glasses in dreams, and reality isn't fading out it's coming into focus as the time creases onto each phase, and the carpet it's not gritty. My eyes are fine and I'm seeing things they way I should see them without the need for some bullshit lens, or some corrective visual aide. My ears tingle, tiny hairs bristle and send the axons dancing toward my brain's integrator, and sense kicks in. Balance. I rub the shaving cream in circles on my cheek. Sense. No sense. I'm supposed to see things with proscribed distortion.

The imbalance of balance and this elusive sensibility keeps slipping and moving and getting peanut brittle crumbly away and I can't find it. The thoughts start falling out of my head onto the bathroom floor and shatter like the steam coats the ideas in a triangle of grammar logic and rhetoric. Think. I don't want to have the order of thoughts. Volition—mine. No no no. I put a finger up to the mirror, but no. I look at my toes, blurred with blue steam and it's all go. I step into the shaving cream. Shower's still running. Back in the dream-zone. They're waiting for me. Never left, it's their home. Do they have the same carpeting? I can ask, I can talk, but no words don't need em not here in another dimension. The DreamZone.

18

NACERIMA TRIBE

The holes in time were there fifty-thousand years ago, but who cared? XY and XX's lives had to be lived. Berries gathered, Antelope clubbed. Life on the Kalahari went on day after month after year. Lives were lived, children bred, circles of humans formed—all the subjects of their own biology.

"Cultural Realism?" CP said authoritatively.

"How can you NOT be biased if you're part of something? Who are the Nacerima and Latipso and how are these Nacerima functioning as they do? Grinder asked.

Is it: Biochemical Slavery? CP added.

“What're you, paranoid”

“When did Noah build the arc?” CP asked.

“He built it before the rain dummy.”

“You're sayin' some shit's going down.”

“Do I have to?” CP said.

“My Amygdala's gone orange.”

“The fuck?” Grinder said.

“Stress man, fucking stress.”

“What're you shy?”

“No asshole. I don't give a shit if someone rates, grades, or compares. I might get shot.”

“The neurons of the paraventricular nucleus of my hypothalamus are tingling. Corticotropin and arginine vasopressin are hittin' my hypophyseal portal system and spanking my locus ceruleus hard.”

“It's a pons thing.” Grinder said.

“Yeah, my fucking brain stem, and I'm tuning it down.” CP said.

“You can do that?”

“You can too Grinder. I've got the heebie jeebies.”

“Heebie friggin' jeebies?” Grinder's lids narrowed. “The fuck you talkin' about CP?”

“The fantods.”

“—the fuck?”

“Anxiety man. Can you dig that?”

“I can. Let's have a friggin' drink.” Grinder reached into a pocket unscrewed the top of a hip flask and took a drink. “Pappy CP, Pappy Van Winkle,” he said and held it up.

CP took the container looked at it and said: “May you live as long as you want and never want as long as you live.”

“Same to you pal. Like the man said: 'The people trying to make this world worse never take a day off' dig THAT.”

“I can dig it Grinder. Good stuff.”

“Pappy or Bob Marley?”

“Both,” CP said. “I'll have another.”

“Me too.” Grinder said just as the phone rang.

“You gonna pick that up?”

He shrugged and looked at the ancient device. “I don't know.”

19

Finding Things Out When You're Not Looking For Anything

“Well, well,well, here we are again with a quirk. Something was found which should best have remained unfound.”

“What do you mean Doc?” CP asked.

“Another hiccup in history that needs to be fixed”.

“What if things just played out?” Grinder added.

“We might . . .” Doc Beaufort held out his hand palm up, and closed it into a fist. Opened it again quickly and and blew at it, finally saying: “Poof we disappear.”

“Accidents happen.” CP said.

“Do you know how they really found out that there were missiles in Cuba all those years ago?”

“Cuba, missiles, I don't—”

“It was the Twentieth Century and could have been a nuclear war. What happened back then was that there were American spy plane photos of regular surveillance. The pictures were reviewed by the spy service and nothing really showed much. Oh, the pictures were passed down the line from one 'expert' to another all saying yeah yeah there's nothing there, and gave them to a file clerk to put away. The clerk was just about to file the pictures in that 'nothing' file, and looked at them. She technically wasn't authorized to look, but nonetheless she did.” Doc Beaufort said.

“Was she one of us?” Grinder said.

Doc Beaufort held up his hand and continued. “The file clerk said: 'Wait a second fellas, did you see this?' To the dismay of the spy masters the clerk said that the pictures depicted soccer fields, and pointed out loudly that the Cubans were not soccer players rather baseball aficionados. All of the CIA agents agreed and the Russians were plucked out as setting up nuclear missiles to attack America."

"You thwarted a nuclear war." CP said.

"At that time."

"We truly do not have time for this folderol."

"No, we don't. This trivial nonsensical fuss is designed I believe, to deplete our assets." Grinder said.

"No my dear boys, it is to misdirect us."

20

HIDING OUT IN THE TEEN YEARS OF THE TWENTIETH CENTURY

May-Li Gets Her Start In Another Time Another Place

May-Li had nothing to do. Nada. Her husband was having an affair. Divorce, cash settlement, and a place to live. She bought a condo, paid cash—his cash, and she pissed it away day trading.

The dot-com bubble came and she'd blown it all. Had to refi her condo. Eh, no big deal everyone was doing it, and this was the right time and the right place. She lived at a condo in Florida, South Florida. Maybe she could find another meal ticket.

Not a bad looking broad, right? She figured. "Make myself marketable, get a real estate license, give that a whirl, maybe do interior decorating too, they're all fags not a hot babe like me? Hey, there's bank in that right? No such luck. Maintenance due every quarter at the condo, stupid place! If I could lower the fees that'd be cool, but I gotta do a refi. Yeah get some bank, pay some bills down. Not pay them off-fuck that. Who pays anything off in full. Nobody paid me in full for anything. I spent all those years married to asshole and he leaves me for another woman? Fuck that, he owes me. Fuck it. I got bills to pay and no one to fuck. I owe my charge cards big time, but I'm just gonna make minimal monthlies. Then stiff em."

"This is Florida, USA, so anyone can get away with anything, and it all shitty shit shit if you play cards right. May-Li good card player. Royal Flush for me. They'll send the collection shit for a while then sell the debt to some collection agency and they'll call over and over and over, and then say fuck it and sell it again till they the debt's whittled down to pennies on the dollar, dig?"

"Yeah, then I can settle all hinky dinky debt for two cents on the dollar if I FEEL like it. Why even pay them at all. I'll put everything into my cousin

Mu Chow's name, yeah. Fuck that shit. I stiffed the charge card companies for maybe two, three hundred K and still got to pay maintenance, mortgage, and car payment. I got to get a refi again. Shit, I get cash advance. Big big big. Yeah. Ten months later all money gone. Shit shit. I got to cut the expenses down. What to do what to do? Oh yeah, I get idea."

"Maybe get on the condo board of directors or some bullshit like that, hook up with some players, make some whoopee, maybe get hitched to some fogey who'll pay my bills. Yeah. Found a dentist on the board start into the hot and heavy but the wife goes apeshit. Fuckin' A. They split but he's president of the board and this condo has some serious bank."

"May-Li have to find a gig. What to do what to do. I got smart idea I run for president of board. All men like me, they love me, they want sucky sucky. I get on board and lower fees for maintenance. Maybe see good idea make money here. I get idea maybe have outside company do billing of maintenance and whoever here no get control of money. No no. Too many questions and no big room makey deal. I see how this work. Bing bang six months go I see how board operate. Looky looky bang bang."

"Board has ability to hire manager to get good paycheck. I likey like that gig. I use my cutey cutey to get gig. Yep that work good. Everyone love May-Li. May-Li get nice gig as president of board. I charm socks off everyone. I no likey like pay bills so hire company to make bills. I hire Jinky CPA in Tallahassee. They far away no see nothing but what I send Jinky. I smart with money I show other board members how smart May-Li is and get good deals. I know real estate interior design and I get free lawyer as part of my new job. Oh May-Li have fun make money and live nice life. I get this that and all May-li wants. I get to pick and choose good contractors who want work for May-Li."

"May-Li no getting younger—need money. No more nail salon no more nicey nice to little girls and old lady people with plastic nails. No more. Need opportunity. Like that word 'opportunity' remind me of how we dig tunnels in 70s and chop chop Yankee Doodle in home land. All those years look like lines on face. Some day May-Li get all youthful and fit again. They can do anything in USA with the Botox and plastic surgery and there big shot Yankee Doodle live right here. I talk. I talky talk talk and let Yankee Doodle doctor see my fine fine body, and he say that if time comes and May-Li need something maybe make nice deal. Not ready yet not enough money. But I know time is moving fast fast fast. Fate they say in my country sometime blows in like magic. Ok, I wait for magic."

21

THE BIG BLOW

“Hurricane comes to Florida. Big damage to condo. Big big damage to this stinky rinky dink ass head. Yankee Doodles never see shit but they panic like B-52's dropping big bombs. May-Li see opportunity!”

“I got all money from residents every quarter to bank and not enough to pay for fixy fix. We got condo insurance for all property five hundred units. I get money I control and I can make my board of director go along with my thinky think. They love May-Li. May-Li go have party party with board of director and we stay real tight.”

“May-Li know how to make deals.”

"I get vendors makey bids. I get best of best. Big money dollars. I show board fancy nicey nice things. Board say okay May-Li. We vote. Okay May-Li you get board approved for this and that. Yippee May-Li get pay check and maybe little extra."

"I find Fancy Company for fixy fix roof. They bid, and want one million USD and they do ALL work. Supplies, equipment, materials, supervision, their own worky worky mans. All professional people work for roof company. Okay I say and tell board and board say okay okay. They vote but May-Li know board say okay. Have money come in every quarter from 500 residents some go to 'maintain' okay okay. But need more so I move one from column A to column B and tell roof company they get job. I makey down payment and roof company bring supplies. I get all supplies and looky looky all there. Roof company deliver all goodies, I inspect. And bing bang boom I got all set up. Roof company want money. I got all the goodies I say fuck you roofy roof people. I got my own people do this installation. Ha."

"I already get the money one million USD from a special assessment to the 500 residents. Plus I take few hundred thousand dollar from people who collect maintenance Jinky CPA Company in

Tallahassee. They easy. May-Li just call Jinky CPA and they give May-Li money for any work I say need be done, and call it maintenance or operating expenses. Nobody know what May-Li use for because that May-Li business. May-Li know this."

"Nobody check the books in May-Li office because all books are clean as May-Li coolie hole."

"Now I get big money and no pay contractor. This too easy. I get bids I say okay okay you get job. Board say okay. I get supply and equipment best of best and say fucky fucky you. They want money for work and install, paint this, fix that. Blah blah I say to lawyer who work for May-Li to say fucky fucky off. Letters, petitions? May-Li no available."

"I have real good secretary she say to everyone May-Li no here. I no answer phone. I no pay bills. I get calls from board of director people and May-Li sit them down and say looky looky we no have to pay these people because May-Li have people she work with do real cheap. Real cheap and money left over. Chop chop no big deal I help you, you help me."

"May-Li like board because May-Li do special good things for special friends help May-Li. Maybe some rubba dubba maybe some extra loan or some worky worky. May-Li have special jobs for special people. May-Li love new job. I hire workers to come and go. I hire guards to protect all supply I order. Nobody come and nobody ask question because all books are clean and pure from Jinky CPA. All squeaky clean. Any questions from vendors to May-Li go to lawyer they go fuck themselves cause May-Li know people settle for penny on dollar. May-Li love this business."

"New car new boys new friends. This going to be a good gig for May-Li."

"Things go real nice for next few years. May-Li collect funds from all 500 go to Jinky. May-Li call Jinky say she need money for computer. No problem. May-Li money for this, no problem. May-Li ask for money for tiki tiki and no problem. This too easy. May-Li need big job need more workers. Some workers asky too much question. Too many complaints from old vendor old people say they pay too little."

"Make trouble for May-Li. May-Li make them look like poopy. Fuck with May-Li fuck with all, so May-Li collect more money, get sent to Jinky and Jinky give report. One of May-Li friend want special favor and May-Li say okey dokey and she bring special landscaper for pet project. May-Li say okey dokey and call Jinky for money."

"Somebody see this and make big trouble, tear up contract say go fucky fucky. Win some lose some. Send money every quarter to Jinky and May-Li spend for you. You love May-Li she trusty. May-Li keep you place okay with special favors and workers and let you use lawyer for your trouble if you not give May-Li trouble. May-Li got boyfriend need work. May-Li give job. May-Li no asky question to boyfriend."

"May-Li hire vendors and stiff them and have lawyer who make them settle for pennies. Ha. Dumb Yankee Doodles."

"May-Li have plenty workers who can do all work. Fire if they ask questions and take money out of one of many accounts to pay for this or that and nobody know because May-Li no tell Jinky CPA, they not know nothing. Only know May-Li hard worker get best of best and make all look real nice May-Li love you all day."

"May-Li get pay first everybody wait. Fuck you. May-Li buy nice car, nice clothes, get maybe tummy tuck. Pay for boy toy and all sort of fun. May-li live large."

"Any question? Fuck you. Nobody fuck with May-Li. May-Li survive Vietnam. May-Li victim. Sick too. Big trouble. May-Li have plenty help prove how sick May-li be. BUT, May-Li find way to get out of this dumpy dump dump. Some Yankee Doodle say he make deal with May-li, make May-Li feel real well in body and in pocketbook and bail from this place. May-Li meet big shot doctor who say he knows way to do funny funny not haha funny business and I get clean new person new life like when May-Li leave Vietnam. He say he can—for the right 'special assessment' get me whole new life. Not want cut other people in. May-Li know the wind is blowing bad winds, and maybe time for trip to meet man with red Cadillac convertible. He say he make all cool for me and not tell nobody—I just show up at some funny ticky tacky strip mall in middle of nowhere and he do magic. Magic? Hahaha I say, but this Yankee Doodle have something special and say May-Li never say word, just go along."

"Right now the heat is on for May-Li here, and it time for boogie. Jail no place for May-Li. Big choice, huh? Jail and lawyers maybe big trouble or trust—I hate that word—TRUST. This Elvis pelvis Yankee Doodle. Big choice, trust or bust."

22

WHY SETTLE IN 1958? DOC BEAUFORT CONTINUES HIS EXPLANATION TO CP

Doc Beaufort spoke to CP in no uncertain terms about the Defense Advance Research Agency.

“DARPA CP, that's one of the reasons Milly and I came to Hoogerstown way back when. We had a place to assure ripples in specific-time did not occur.”

“I know a little bit about it, but not much.” CP said.

“Some folks in the name of 'National Security' used NLP, or Neurolinguistic Programming to stratify large portions of the population in the US.”

"How?"

"A salient feature was the use of programming via television, radio, and motion pictures."

"What were the origins?" CP asked.

"In 1945, Ultra the CIA's mind control program began with OPERATION PAPERCLIP, which brought >1500 Nazi scientists to the US. Among MLK Ultra's usage was sound: RF sound via Dr. Ross Adey, using Amplitude Modulation of theta rhythms thus creating a mass hypnosis that remained throughout the early part of the 21st Century."

"Social engineers eh? Techniques to control populations."

"Yes CP. In fact this was described by HG Wells, as akin to arenas put up around the world for sports."

"It didn't really work out as planned, did it?"

"No CP, it only served a fragment of the earth's population, and less of that of the US. Because humans exist as tribal systems."

“And a tribal system establishes that the average man disengages, right?”

“Yes, yes indeed, to tend to the needs of their own tribes. However, for many there were few tribes to embrace within their own lives.”

“Hamster wheeling through life. Always something, but there were outlets, weren't there?”

“Of course. For many the outlets of their day to day life resulted in gradual helplessness. Have them engage in following a sport or team they can cheer on using radio to broadcast, and people live vicariously. Not living their own lives.”

“A culture industry with 'Cultural Leaders' and renewable material. Uploads and upgrades. Today we have 'political correctness’ and we bounce ideas off friends and peers who have had same or similar information.”

“Mind control at it its best.” Beaufort said.

“Ask dumb questions and you're ostracized. Only concern yourself with death, taxes, and using sleep deprivation via shoddy mass dietary manipulations leading to dehydration. Who would recognize anomalies of the daily ten percent potassium loss? No one." CP said.

"An interesting note on one among many ways this ploy failed is this: Try to sell vaseline in Europe -that's gasoline. Verboten!"

"CP, the Time Bureau is to assure the conspiracy theories, mind control, and nonsense causes minimal damage to the flow of history. There is one axiom for those of us with the Bureau."

"Hang on Beaufort, are you saying they own you? An abundance of crime linked to pollution?"

"Industrial discharge of lead and manganese, much from the chemical trails of an emerging airline industry." Beaufort said."

"Headlines persist though."

"There are patterns of imbeciles getting ready to overthrow their own government."

"I've read about a few."

"How about this one CP? Operation 'BAJINKO'?"

“A conspiracy theory regarding the 911 attacks, that claimed it was an inside job. They didn't evacuate any other buildings. They didn't hit Chicago or the Standard Oil building.”

“It was one among many, so-called conspiracy theories from the Templar Treasures, King Solomon's Mines, the Lost Cities, and on and on developed by us time travelers?”

“In 2070 we set out to cleanse peoples minds of different eras. To ask questions, develop curiosities, and single out folks who could reach outside the mind control gibberish. And you CP, and that cretin —I say it fondly, he's a good man—to look beyond yourselves. Ask questions, ask ask ask, and suspect everything, question the very fabric of reality. The conspiracy theories were merely planted to break apart complacency, idiocy, and the damn mass hypnosis that's plagued mankind for so many generations. Hence, the search for duly thoughtful people capable of breaking away—intellectually from what is generated to the masses.”

“What is the axiom?”

“You always let things end in your favor.”

“Via manipulating the DNA code, it's done right?”

“You know this CP. You ARE a physician.” Beaufort said.

“I know, I know: FOUR NUCLEOTIDE BASES make up the rungs of the DNA ladder: Adenine, Guanine, Cytosine, Thymine. Each of these nucleic acids is a letter in the genetic alphabet, AGCT. AG are Purines, TC the pyrimidines. These three letters combined together form three letter 'words'.These letters used in the lingo make up 64 words. They make up the amino acids to be generated in all cells.

“A few thousand years hence the addition of another nucleotide, Mymine was added to the mix. Controlled by supercomputers, always orbiting, and maintaining that no bull pucky occurs.”

“And this way history is preordained.”

“No CP. History and mankind are maintained.”

23

NADINE AND CP 1978

“CP, why are you looking at me that way?” Nadine asked.

“I love you. Don't know how long I've loved you, don't know how long I will. I think of a softness and firmness, and delicacy. Everything comes rushing in my mind like a wave and I see you—not the physical you—the unseeable you-ness of you and feel you blink your soul. God I don't know why I can't shake it off, shrug away this pillar that's standing in my head.”

“That's so sweet.” She reached toward him just as car tires squealed, and doors creaked loudly and slammed hard. She looked over CP's shoulder, it was a van, tinted windows, the side panel open, and dark inside.

CP stood in front of her hands at his sides. What is this? Who are these jokers? He looked at Nadine and the setting sun behind the clouds let out streaks of orange light that made the spray of freckles across her face sparkle like a leopard's spots. Strands of hair caged her face, and her not-quite green, not-quite blue eyes became black as her pupils fully dilated. He could smell the adrenaline being manufactured with each beat of her heart wafting past perfumed carotids. So much for a romantic evening.

Three men darkly dressed—a uniform of sorts—were circling them. Their faces were covered, and they had weapons. What kind of weapons CP couldn't place, but these jokers looked like they'd seen too many movies. He thought they were posing for a 'what tough guys are supposed to look like' scene. More for each other than affect any damage. Finally one spoke: “Yo mo fo freeze you asses!”

CP held his ground as the other two took positions on their right and left. He looked across at the sham commandos. The one who blurted out orders hesitated. They weren't here to shoot anyone.

Frighteners? Did they show up to shake them down, maybe rob them? “You looking for some dough?” CP said.

“Get in the van” he said, his hand was trembling .

“Sure pal, anything you say.” CP held his palms out. “Don't you want me to raise these?”

“I can shoot you now Mofo shoot you dead. Take your bitch.” His voice broke.

“If you were gonna shoot you already would've shot me.”

“Oh yeah mother fucker. I pop a cap in you if don't do what I say.” Tough Guy pulled the trigger and his pistol kicked back. A warning shot. “No one move.”

“Okay, we're comin' pal.” CP lied.

“Yeah. You know we be some trouble.”

“Who's your boss?” CP held both hands up. “Maybe we can work something out.”

“Yo man, I can't go tell you squat man.”

“I can make it worth your while,” CP said.

The kid and former tough guy looked from side to side at his fellow toughies. “What the fuck you got Chalk ain't got mother fucker?”

“Chalk?” CP said. “You work for Chalk?”

“I dint say nothin' man.” Tough guy said, pissed off at himself for ratting out his boss. Gonna have to keep it together next time. Shit, man. “I dint say nothin' man now get you asses in the van.”

“Do as he say,” the man-child to CP holding up his weapon, waving it. “Go,” he said. “I can shoot you in the legs, and you still be fine enough.”

“That wound would bleed like a gusher genius. Your ride would be a mess, and your boss real pissed. The rounds from that,” CP pointed his chin at the rifle, “tear big holes through the flesh.”

“I know dat,” the kid said as if he'd heard it for the first time.

They had modified AKs. The most popular machine gun among `em all. Every third world country had more AK-47s and ammo than food.

“What do you want?” Nadine ordered them—no fear, more of a threat. A threat they couldn't give a rats ass about.

CP held his ground, both arms fanned behind him, shielding his woman. She didn't need shielding because before another word could be spoken, she crouched, rolled, and came up firing a pistol, a very old gun. Two shots and the muzzle flash broke the dusk's mellow—like a thousand fireflies collectively flamed on, syncopated, and let loose a blast of light.

CP looked over at her. He knew the weapon it was a Colt Single Action Army–also known as the Single Action Army, SAA, Model P, Peacemaker, M1873. The Colt .45. A single action revolver with a revolving cylinder that holds six cartridges It was designed for the U.S. government service revolver trials of 1872 by Colt's Patent Firearms Manufacturing Company–and was adopted as the standard military service revolver until 1892, but this gun had been modified, and the ammo in Nadine's gun hand't been invented yet. It wouldn't be for another 250 years.

In a blink she was on her feet, the Colt to the chief pawn's head and her left hand held out in front of him. “I want the keys and instructions to where you're supposed to drive us.”

Before the gunman could answer she ripped the mask from his face and read his thoughts. It was an image he fixed, a place and series of turns on roads he'd memorized.

“I ain't sayin' shit.” He said. “You best go ahead and shoot me lady.” The kid said.

“You're coming with us sports fan.” She said.

“Ain't goin' no place and you don't know but nothin.'” He said.

“Sure she does asshole. We both do.” CP said.

“What're you mind readers? There ain't no map no place.”

“Sure Ramone, sure.”

“How you know my name?”

"You just thought it sports fan." CP said. "So take us to Chalk."

24

CHALK

I know the streets man. Been ridin' my groove twenny year. Know The Man, Man know Chalk. We be cool. I do my thing, they lay low. Why? Your man Chalk always got the skinny on what's goin' down. Somethin' go down I don't like, somethin' not in Chalk's enterprising world, Chalk just dimes the mother-fucker out. In exchange for my kindness T.H.E. Man does not, did I say "does not" cross the Chalk line. They got their yellow DO NOT CROSS tape, and me? I got my DO NOT CROSS CHALK lines. So we be cool. Can you dig it? So how I get to where I'm at? Power baby. I got the power no other brother got. How I get that? I got me the connections. What kind of connections? Ain't no connection folk got `round here, or no place else. I got me a direct line to what gonna happen before it happens. Oh no, don't get no idea Chalk some boo-sheet motherfuck or I bust a cap in you mofo knee.

You see I got me some friends, powerful folk, ain't no white black thing, no. I got me friends who come from the future, uh huh, you heard me right. They pop in now and then and say, Chalk, we take care you, and you take care of folk we send you, dig?

You wanna know how this all go down? Listen up.

Happen few year back: some white folk show up in the hood. Stuck out like whitey do on my turf. I was proppin' up the wall next to the Korean liquor store and the alley—my alley—watchin' one of my ho's doin' some street hustle. I take my eyes off her for a second to light a Kool, and poof—three whitey appear like they been beamed down by Captain Kirk, you dig? Out of thin mother-lovin' air, and dressed for Hallow-Freakin'-Ween, and the mofos ain't got no car. I play this cool, could be a score, or maybe a bust.

My ho, Tamina, she don't look freaked, but shit that bitch always high. Wouldn't see unner cover cop if he was wearin' a uniform.

Tamina be workin' for Chalk six months. Scooped her right off the bus from Peanutville. She got special talent, I pick up on right quck. Tamina, she my number one street ho. Pull in some nice coin with her roadside bj work. Take her but a few minutes to get a horn dog off cause she got no tonsils.

Just pull into the alley, Chalk make sure ain't no freak, pay up, get the fuck out. Every now and then some perv want to play with her titties, and that cost extra. No pay, no play. I just tap my diamond capped cane, and rap on the window. Most John's see me they be cool. Ery now'n-then gotta let my leather badass black coat with Leopard fur collar fall open, see I'm packin, say hello to Mr. Colt, remind Mr. Aggressive who in charge. This be Chalk's alley, dig?

Tamina she good girl, always point me out to her customer I be her boss. Velvet feathered hat, platforms, shades round the clock, especially at night. Oh yeah, I be cool. Ain't never got to bust a cap. Hell no. These boy's lookin' for a street blowser be pussies. They see me lookin' after bidness. Mr. Colt usually just stay nappin' right under my arm. But you can n'er be too sure. Man's got to do what he got to do, dig?

So that day three whitey show up, I just watch.

Funky shit goin' down and I feel Mr. Colt maybe need do some talkin', a language Chalk don't got.

One of the mofos breaks away headed toward me, maybe gonna try cut a deal, maybe they some rich folk want some some kinky suburban shit—which cost extra I might add—and he go past me and says: “Yo my African American brother,” and goes into Korean's store.

What the . . .? I hear the jingles to hip Korea man he got somebody inside the store. Ain't my job to look after his bidnet, less he wanna pay Chalk do some lookin' after, but he got his own people. Whitey in there five minutes already, ain't no sirens, no hollerin' so there must be bidnet, and that means mo-nay. Yeah, and he got to walk right past Chalk. That mofo called me a African. He got some fast dancin' to do, and whitey can't dance for shit. Mofo needs a whoopin', less of course I can extract some capital.

I stay cool. Gots to be cool, dig?

I lay low outside for the mother fucker, maybe mess him up a little bit-maybe not. Me bein' the gentleman of leisure I am, plus there might be a nice score here. Maybe this whitey dressed up like Elvis just some dumbass.

I watch Tamina rap with the tall skinny tan white guy and foxy little gal in some kinda leotard and wait. When I hear the jingle jingle of the liquor store door again.

“Yo my man—” Whitey say.

I push myself away from the wall, “You talkin' to me?” I say.

So I get to rappin' with the dude. Next thing I knew cops are there, and we's in the alley and all kind of shit goin' down. Chalk end up drivin' these three whitey out of Big Town. We get to rap and it all comes out. Blew my mind. They was from the future, and they got me well, I mean some serious well: car, pad, and best of all they supply me with who's who and when's when. So it was a kind of 'symmetry' that what they called it. If I let folk come here and crash whenever I get the call. I don't get no call I don't do but nothin'.

The future people make it real clear there be some strange comin' this way, and I gots to be on the look out. Dig on that, Chalk is the lookout man. I cool with that cause they—the future folks—they be doctors and gonna fix me up in a way I get free doctor I get sick. I ain't sick but I ain't gettin' any younger. Mother fucker who called me a African says he can set me up with shit, make vikes, or percs look like aspirin. Dude says he can hook me up with some enzymes. What the fuck's that? Other cat say they can do some shit to my DNA. The fuck's that? I dint know but for shit `bout that, dint even know I hads it.

Oh yeah they say I do good they set me up right, so I can trip out to the future, or hang out in the old days. Chalk not to cool with bein' a slave, you dig? But the Elvis cat—his real name's Grinder, and the tan whitey CP, and the chicky she be Nadine.

They gonna make shit for Chalk happen. I be their man in 1977. Cool. Maybe they even change the calendar to Chalk year so everybody hear the number 1977 it be Chalk time. I can dig it, says not to worry. Funky thing though, CP wanted to know if I still had my army uniform. Hell yeah, Chalk ain't throw away nothin' especially my badass 101st Airborne threads—hell no. Sergeant at that. Damn I was in `Nam I told him, a decorated solder at that. Um-hmm I been cross the pond. Then CP says—

"Chalk do you know how to steal a car?"

"This some kinda black thing, man? I ought kick your—" I thought he was dissin' me.

"Half a car," he says.

I say, "CP you crazy. Of course I can, but who'd want that?" He just nodded his head, grinned like he done stole somethin' himself, and says my time's comin' for somethin' real big.

That be pretty much how I became a guardian. Make no mistake that ain't no rat or snitch or nothin' like it. I keep a eye on who passes through this year, crazy ass shit don't make no sense at first but they explain. They say in the future folks can travel through some kinda holes—wormholes or portals from one part of history to another. They either got to pay for the privilege, work for The Man, mother fuckin' Man been runnin' shit forever, but now I got me a piece of the action. I cool with it or they be what's called 'interlopers' or time thieves. Mother fucker. I can see how some cats'd play that angle. Kinda like a John usin' one of my hos, usin' my alley, hittin' me up for freebies without payin'.

Future folk tell me I am ideal—like I don't know that—for the job. Shit, this negro knows the streets better than anybody. I'm the man for watchin' and they set me up but good. First thing is they give me this transistor radio lookin' thing with a real small TV screen on it. The foxy chick says I'll get a signal when somebody in my year don't belong here, or is up to what they call 'trouble' and the little screen will have pictures on it.

They spell out what I gotta do: isolate `em, and they say it's cool to use whatever it takes, to me that means Mr.Colt and some homies. They say just press a button and somebody'll come fetch. Pretty fly stuff, dig? They make sure I got all the means necessary—we talkin' a private-mofo-plane, fancy cars, and enough connections I can open up a power plant in the Congo. They say I am a 'gurardian' which they explain is somebody who scopes out folks. Makes sure that somebody who's not supposed to be here is set right, and Chalk checks it out.

They say they can fix any trouble I have with John Q. I'm cool with that in all kinds of ways that go back years before I remember. They say I do good they set me up.

Now let me be clear here, Chalk ain't no dumbass cotton pickin' negro just fell off the turnip truck. I got my sources. I check out this shit, and find out there's shit I never knew could be known. They tole me `bout some shit thass s'posed to be secret, and gonna happen down the road—sho nuff that shit happens. Sportin' games, horse race winners ahead of time.

They got it all down solid. Stock market Wall Street and all that. Shit, I became a wealthy investor off the shit they hipped me to. But make no mistake about it, I knew I walked a thin line. Fuck with these folk and they snuff Chalk like he ain't never been born. That's when it occurred to me that they NEEDED me, more than I needed them. At first I couldn't figure it, but if I wasn't me who'd do dat shit? No no no, I had to be a part of some big picture and knew some how some way I was gonna find out, and that my brothers and sisters was gonna be Chalk's big score. Can you dig it?

So bidness as a guardian goes good. Turns out cool as cool can be for a spell, somebody shows up, I pop in and let `em know who boss, and some other future folk shows up and they be gone. I don't axe no questions. It started to get so routine I hired on some boys do patrollin' for me. Chalk a busy man, dig? So today I get this message on the box, and send my boys out, and things went down funky. It started when I call my homie Ramone.

25

RAMONE

I can't cool down. Crazy ass bitch make me nuts. I be in the shower hear a boom boom boom. Maybe the P S at the door. What the fuck? I turn off the H2O or keep it flowin'? P S is hip to that shit. Write down perp is evading service-not cool. Judge see that go nuts. Say I beese on the DL hard, come back again. Shit. I cleans myself and cool out of the room. Bitch is yellin at some shit or another. I'm thinkin' some heat, maybe some other shit go down. Nada. Crazy ass bitch look like Q-tip hair up in towel sayin' she want her shampoo. Turn out she be odin' the stomp stomp. Shit. What the—

"Yo woman, what you doin'"?

She go all nutso on my ass. Some bullshit not wantin' to disturb my 'privacy'.

Bitch just sucked my cock and she worried about my privacy? What kinda sense that make? Shit. She goes into a lecture about her routine. What the fuck routine. You need some shit you go in the room and you get the shit. She changes her rap to the lighting. The fucking lighting in the other bathroom? What the fuck. This bout common-fucking-sense. I go fucking ballistic on this, ain't nobody this wacked out less they got some brain worm crawlin' between logic and conditioner-hair fucking conditioner. Shit. Now she just sit there ain't say but for nothin' I don't get it. The phone rings.

“Ramone you gonna answer dat?” She say.

“I don't say boo.”

“You gonna say somethin' Elena?” I axe.

The phone on the tenth ring. I grab it. “Whassup Chalk?”

“My bitch is havin' a fit jefe, wha you want me to do?”

"What does that man want now, steal a car? You were a great mechanic, but no you got to run with hoodlums."

"Hush up Elena. I gotta take Chalk someplace."

"Where?"

"Don't go askin' no questions woman."

Maybe I ought not've been so loud cause she got the question mark over her head and watched me put on my work clothes, arms folded under her tits, shakin' her head. Bitch don't care where the money comes from then just like that she gets to wonder? No, man. I got to get a couple guys to help me with this shit. Can't have her listenin' to my phone calls. Chalk go nuts he know somebody else know his business. Marone the broad's gonna get me killed. She's watchin' me check my gun, the ski mask. Shit. This is not lookin' good.

"Where you goin' now some chop shop? You some marícon crook now? You could've—"

"Girl you mind your face" I say, feel my skin getting hot. I could strangle this bitch. Shit don't ask no focking questions.

"Ramone you got to stop running with these people." Elena had both hands on her hips.

"You like this place, those clothes, the apartment? Everything we got is cause Chalk brought me in."

"In to what? You want to get locked up. Again?" She stood in front of the apartment's door.

"Elena get out of my way, I got to take care of things or—"

"Or what. That colored guy is going to do what, that the police won't do? Look at you," she stepped back. "You're dressed like a soldier, carry a pistol, and you're stinking draft dodger. And those hoodlums you run with?"

"You're in my way Elena I got to go."

"I'm seek of your sheet Ramone. Sick sick sick of it."

I took my roll of bills out and started counting out hundreds. Bitch grabbed the wad of cash and tossed it at me. I can't lose it man. I can't let this happen. Can't keep Chalk waiting, and this shit? I can't think right. “Elena we'll talk about it when I get back.”

“Maybe I won't be here Ramone. Maybe I just be finished with this life.”

“Elena please—” I was tucking my gun in its holster when she opened the door.

“Just go. Every time that phone rings I don't know. Every time there's a knock on the door, I don't know. I can't live like this, I can't.”

I took out my gun, it was warm in my hand. She looked at me look at my pistol. Her eyes wide, what the fuck? What am I fucking doing? I opened the door and ran. Ran out to the van waiting downstairs with two guys in it. We had to go meet some fuckers. Oh shit, what's going on? This is some fucked up shit. I got to have a sit down. I gotta take Chalk for a ride, some cornfield out in the boonies.”

26

EDDY ASK: WHAT THE HELL?

Busted in some funky third world land yet to be visited by modern dentistry. Shit on a fucking stick what am I doing here? Got to mellow out—pop a V. Valium ten would do just fine. I break it in half and look up. Shit where am I? Some cafeteria in yo yo land? Fucking army headquarters for some revolutionaries or shit like that?

I'm sitting at a picnic table, and some Ashley in a shabby camo uniform with some old fashioned rifle is watching us eat—Us? Who the fuck are these people around me? Shit they've got no faces. They're quiet, not chattering, just their heads down.

27

THE RANDOMNESS OF ENTROPY AT EDDY'S NEW DIGS

There is chaos among unit owners where once there was centralized communication. Data streaming from a singular source—Management.

The elected board of directors have remained the sole source for years. Why? What motivates the same characters who—as we're told—have no financial interest in being on the board other than the same because we say so mumbo jumbo again and again.

A few rocks have been turned over, and some grimy material's surfaced. It ain't pretty. What material, what documents, what photos, why, who, where, when? These unknowns are now knowns, and despite admonitions of rebellion the real players in this mini-fiefdom are one by one being exposed as complicit in a smoothly run, maximum deniability, profitable endeavor, for a select group of folks who've found this place to be easy pickin's for too long.

By simply maintaining absolute control of communications and financial data, not the sanitized CPA offerings, to the tune of paint drying. The "other" set of books stays where it belongs—in the hands of those profiting off the unit owners.

Sure it looks all nicey nice, legit and all, but once the folks—unit owners that is—take to talking among themselves: "massah ain't got but nothin' to say." The field negros who've paid their dues are reading who gets paid what, why, and how they're connected. Massah ain't happy.

Now massah gonna have to be held accountable, and they don't like it. Maybe massah been cookin' the books.

May-Li been on the DL since the condo scam. Big trouble. Everything was good then, everything go bad. Back to the nail business.

Everyone wanted something or another.

That chick May-Li ups and disappears, and that Burt “Winner” Winn? Who the fuck are these people and what's their freaking flipped out freakazoid agenda? Who knows how that'll get me screwed up?

Eddy needed to talk to someone, and his first choice was Grinder. He needed to set things right in his mind, and maybe find out how long he'd be stuck at this place.

“Hey Eddy, what's up?” Grinder said.

“How'd you know I was going to call?”

“I'm a regular Johnny-on-the-spot guy Eddy. I know shit before it friggin' happens, dig? I know you're freaked man, but don't worry. Just chill I'll hang with you when I get back.”

“Back from where?”

Grinder said, “Doc Beaufort and crew said they need me to show up at the Battle of this or the signing of that, some bullshit event or another.”

“Great.” Eddy said.

“Listen Eddy, time travel isn't for everyone. Space and time and all that razzmatazz were makin' me crazed. I didn't know where I'd be or when I'd be there, and shit was coming at me like you wouldn't believe.”

“So I'm complicit in whatever happens? I have to develop, spin, play, exploit this, work that. Shit, time traveling's not for me, Grinder.”

“Eddy, sometimes it gets to me too. For me it sucks, but the perks are great. Trust me, I'd rather be sitting at a bar instead of visiting some dictator, bank robber, stock market manipulator, this, that or some other portal hopper. Dig?”

“Not really,” Eddy said.

“Just sit tight.” At that Grinder was gone.

28

TESSELATED EDDY

The world got all sort of fucked since I've been sleeping. I don't know what happened—did folks go nuts? Wars here, wars there, everybody done whomped each other for no apparent reason. Maybe there be some cash, some booty, some good dope. I get to thinking it ain't nothing that people want they ain't wanted once before. Titties look the same they always done. Food taste just as it did, smokes be the same, and liquor get you the same buzz. Must be some static electricity in the air makes folks go nutty and kill each other. How many farms can a guy have.

I need to have some action. Eddy said to himself.

Sex is a good thing, and it's clinically proven to have salubrious effects. The ingredients in semen include mood enhancers like estrone, cortisol, oxytocin, prolactin, serotonin, plus the sleep enhancer melatonin, and, of course sperm (1%-5%.). Delivering these compounds into the richly vascularized vagina has major salutary effects for the recipient.

Part of the continuity of a balanced life, sex on a regular basis is imperative. Don't even consider it again. You screw, you shit, shower, shave, or whatever you do to get on with your day. If you've got that itch that goes unscratched, trust me on this, you'll have a shitty day. So there, that's that. Go take care of business.

When Eddy awoke from suspended animation the world had gone through several iterations of itself. Decades passed, people died, and others born, grown, and became what they would.

Ordinary human life went on to the extent that was appropriate to the times. However, at his awakening the world looked nothing like the one he left. His induced cessation from humanity was not punitive, no, rather a preventive measure because Edward Cash witnessed events during the course of his lifetime that would at some time alter his behavior, thus causing events to occur which would be considered nonconforming, or out-of-synch with the overall scheme of things.

Unfortunately Eddy chanced upon a series of events inconsistent with his world view which were so profound he took it upon himself to intervene. This intervention would have disrupted the overall sequence of those events, thus disrupting what had to occur to maintain the natural order of things. One person cannot—according to forces outside this narrative—in any way alter, change, or modify the fabric of any given reality. Disruptions of the fabric of time because of an accidental tear in the material, which by the way were not "accidents" at all, rather unintentional tessellations in the layers of existence as accounted for by human consciousness.

29

KNOWABLE THINGS (REFLECTIONS OF DOC BEAUFORT)

If everything knowable is reduced to a deck of cards, then on any given plane of that knowable reality the characters on those cards can be shuffled, dealt, and flipped over in any number of knowns and unknowns. If you take that deck of cards, and consider the surface of each as a Möbius strip—a finite unidimensional entity onto itself—and pulse through any one among those cards a force unlike any in that known universe a disruption occurs.

Thus effecting all the cards, in all the decks in all the layers of history in a universe held together with much more than the paperclips, glue, and chewing gum. This is not restricted to maintaining any particular knowable realm. Things, generally get fouled up in ways not only unimaginable, but out-of-control desynchronizing the flow of history.

30

DAMES DUKING IT OUT

When a "trusted" friend goes bonkers and does something so stupidly malicious you've got to bang your brain against the inside of your skull and say: "What the hell." Eddy lamented.

Of course you'll never get why they'd commit acts of assholery, but it'll eat away at you like some weaselly vermin from a bad cartoon. Sure Wylie Coyote is expected to do some funky shit, but someone you trust and believe's a friend? C'mon, what the fuck's going on here aside from the usual: "broads are freaking nuts!" You never really get it, and you wonder, and you theorize, and come up with all sorts of reasons still trying to defend this so-called "pal" only to find the innards of your skull bounced further around until you just sit back and say: “What a piece of shit.”

You see, this sort of business is almost endemic to chicks—”broads” if you will, because women do some very fucked up stuff for no apparent reasons other than it's in their nature. Hormones? Eh, maybe. But driving yourself nuts over a dumb ass chick fucking over another chick can be hazardous to your sanity—which by the way you lost when you thought you could put much stock in the reliability of a self-serving broad. So there it is in a nutshell, a damn crummy one too—probably stale at that.

31

He had a constipated cow to deal with. Joe Aberton's bovine beast was puffed up from paralyzed portions of her digestive domain. Despite each and every remedy—some graphically grotesque, foul and messy—this Holstein-Friesian wasn't going to let loose no matter what. She kept getting larger.

After a week she'd doubled in size. Joe knew there was some off-the grid, former carnie folks called upon from time to time for odd jobs. This was about as odd in Joe's world as things could get.

Joe called upon a man known for leaving the scene of an accident and smuggling bootleg boner drugs from Canada claiming his truck was stolen.

Elmo Kumberbach hand't used a telephone in over a year, which, is about equal to the amount of time he'd spent in and out of various penal institutions, so Joe was a bit skeptical about calling on him for this awkward situation.

In fact Mrs. Aberton, also known as Abbey said: "Joe, either get that worthless cow off the farm, or I'll shoot her myself." Which, of course she would. This nonproductive dairy cow was taking up too much time and space, as well as vet bills, and all the other expenses. "That cow's no darn good Joe." Abbey said every day thus disrupting the natural order of the Aberton's good life. After all, it's not easy running a working farm. Joe was attached to this cow for no known rhyme or reason. He just wasn't ready to let old Bessy go, at least without going—after all they could use the fertilizer, and they'd already gone through who knows what to care for the critter.

Elmo Kumberbach lived in a 1965 Airstream Tradewind he'd won in a card game. It may have been old, dirty, rotting, and smelly, but to Elmo, this was home sweet home. He had the shiny silver land yacht nestled in a thicket over at the National Park far from view from any ranger who might suggest this vehicle may very well be trespassing.

Elmo's ingenuity in evading law enforcement after that “false arrest”—his truck really was stolen. It came in handy camouflaging the trailer, and gave him and his monkey the seclusion they needed to keep things just so. Just so Elmo could breed his collection of reptiles: snakes, lizards, and who knew what to concoct his “special formulas” for sale when all else failed. Elmo had developed a career based on his manufactured lineage as a genuine half Cherokee, part Apache, fully trained by tribal elders “medicine man” or, if the situation arose for a higher credential it was Elmo K, Shaman. He liked the sound of it, and so did the marks, or in carnie-speak, rubes.

The same folks who'd try getting a coin to stick to a Pam sprayed pan for a stuffed animal would pay plenty for some potion or lotion that no civilized healer—even the most crooked of crook chiropractors could cook up. Elmo had his own special blend. He used science by having his friend, companion, and perhaps other less than thinkable relations with monkeys. Sample it prior to selling a batch of one of his products. Maybe some day he'd find out who stole his truck, and give that rat bastard a dose.

32

DAPHNE

Chip was still with the blonde, all dolled up sipping Champagne. Oozing that “look at me look at me” thing, and then pouting about all the men raping her with their eyes. He wasn't only on to her bullshit, but for five grand a night this pussycat best know what's new, and it ain't the Cartier on his wrist. He was sick and tired of running this do-nothing “escort” that wanted more than what she was worth. Customers were complaining, and the heat was hanging heavy every time he set up a date with this ho. Fuck.

Sure he screwed her, he screwed all his bitches—even bought this one a new car. Had to keep things looking legit, but he was going to cut her loose tonight. Too damn dumb to deal with.

33

AS EDDY WOULD SAY: BROADS

I gotta tell you when chicks–oh please let me phrase this politically correct (yeah right)–they get in arguments that turn into full blown stress-a-thons, and vector in on every "button" to push to piss each other off. There's no rhyme, reason, grammar, logic, or rhetoric that makes sense out of what I call "chick talk" but it happens. And this shit goes on and on and on, and gals of ALL freaking ages get some "issue" in their heads and don't let go. Like mad freakin' mutts making up some new way to chase their own tails.

Young, old, middle age, whatever. When two (or more) women get in some dumb ass argument—which usually is about nothing—they NEVER let go till one of them cries, gets emotionally addled, or goes screwy. I've seen it bros, truly witnessed the craziness of broads. There are no rules, just ridiculous admonitions of wackiness that have no bearing in any known galaxy. What the fuck's with that? Do homos do that shit? Gay marriage? Like super chicks on steroids or some other wacko drug. They duke it out in their own catty ways. Excuse the discrediting of cats, but once you've seen a couple broads go at it over what most dudes would consider a bad shit—the no toilet paper thing—you gotta wonder if there's some funky femme fandango. I dig broads, but I swear to you I never want to listen to a couple chicks beef it out, dig? They go around and around and avoid the salient points, it's always some ancillary bullshit that's got nothing to do with the main event, that being what the fuck are you bitches fighting over? A misunderstanding? Blah.

I propose a new dictionary on chicks that describes the how to's of what the fucks, so dudes don't get all zipped out on what the fuck the chicks are all ferbigitated about. Good luck with that, right! Seeing as how broads control what gets published where, when, and by who. Man oh man just square off and play it straight. Say it as you see it and play it as it lays.

Your pal Eddy

Oh yeah, there's this: when dudes play the chick scene and play chick fight. Dudes who get caught up in acting like beefing broads are pretty much either low on testosterone, a decent bonable bone, or just man-bee yatches. So if you rap with a dude who's gotten himself into a chick fight you ask yourself this: “What the fuck is with this he-she man bitch, eh?

Ask Eddy about these mondo-chick weirdos. I don't get involved with chick on chick shit because women can work shit out on their own and don't need some dude with a man-gina.

34

A CHIP OFF THE OLD BLOCK

Unbeknownst to anyone Chip really wasn't "Chip" at all. He was Abdul El-something or other, and wasn't too straight a shooter on any battlefield. That's why Chip: after failing bad-guy training in a certain Persian Gulf nation as an up and coming carrier of all sorts of mayhem to the Western World was selected to use one of the many "Kingdom's" resources to establish front businesses in America. None of which by the way did very well at all bringing the wrath of a certain sheik to kindly request his removal.

Aside from owning an exotic car repair shop in Fort Lauderdale, Florida, Squeaky Wheels LLC, Chip's holdings were at best confusing. The Rolls and Bentley set considered the shop among the finest, others not so fine at all—rather a chop shop, scam, or money laundering pit to wash and wax loot from dubious dealings. If putting BBs in car doors to add that: “What's that sound” was considered a legit business ploy, they'd be clean as clean can be, but they weren't. A few thousand dollars of auto diagnostics often resulted in small ball removal, wash, and maybe a little spray of oil on an otherwise fine engine part.

Squeaky Wheels LLC was just “home base” or the command center for Chip's enterprise, which he built up in in late 2012. An established business entity in Florida by most definitions is any company that's been in business longer than eight months. At the time, 2014, the boys, actually young men, give or take five years were pillars of the community.

In fact, one well heeled customer was so impressed with work done on his Bentley—repair of his car's clock—the Breitling in the dash was off, and the boys switched it out for a fugazi. That worked swell, the customer Miles Bannister, publisher, billionaire, wrote them up on every online review site, and featured them in one of his glossy, stylish, chi chi magazines.

They were a local phenomenon, true superstars, to the wealthy in automotive need. They were also rumored to do “special favors” for some preferred—as in cash paying—customers. Some “favors” were not so wholesome by legal standards. However, the cousins were riding the wave of good fortune.

Chip and his first cousin, a man known to all who knew him, but who really knows anyone—as The Corporal. The cousins, had holdings, or so they claimed in five cigar bars, and an off—very off—shore petroleum company. Chip and his cousin also had a stake in a pharmaceutical company in Honduras which, coincidentally was equipped with authentic hand made cigar manufacturers.

Rumors among those who've had the displeasure of dealing, in any capacity, with the cousins were collectively on the same page as having a similar bad taste in their mouths which often required massive amounts of Listerine, Scope, and several shots of strong ethyl alcohol. The dubious task of cancelling all their charge cards, reporting a “missing identity” and always, several dollars lighter.

When Eddy C, MD Plastic Surgeon Extraordinaire pulled into—

35

GRINDER TELLS CP . . .

“Life has become immeasurably better since I have been forced to stop taking it seriously.”~Hunter S Thompson.

I dig that quote. Why? I used to take every friggin' thing as serious as if was life or death. Then again there is that part of my life when everything WAS life or death; when I was a practicing physician.

Those days long slipped away after CP dragged me through that rabbit hole, into the bizarro space-time continuum, and I met all these freaks from the past and the future. Dig?.

“Uh, Grinder, 'I DRAGGED YOU?' cut the shit.”

"All right, all right WE got dragged—"

"More like you conned me into going to a nursing home with you to see patients. We got run off the road and into a cornfield by some wacked out eighteen-wheeler, gassed by a crop duster, and woke up in 1958. Remember that?" CP said.

"To tell you the truth CP I didn't know you were here." Grinder said.

"You're so full of crap Grinder."

"That nursing home would have made us both some nice bank."

"We both know that wasn't meant to be, and we'd both be dead—or worse—if that happened."

"Meh, maybe so. I did dig 1978 or was it '77?"

"I thought you were going to stay back there with the pimp, Chalk, and his number one ho Tamina."

"You fell for a broad from 2070. How's that gig going?"

"Fine Grinder, just fine. So here we are in . . . What year is this?"

"Do I look like a calendar?"

"Shut the fuck up Grinder. Beaufort summoned us."

"Summoned? Ooh fancy phrasing CP. He needed us here to do some frigging shit. Him and that dame Milly. They're in some kind of jam, people jumping in and out of the wrong times and shit."

"Serious shit."

"Hey CP how's my hair look?"

"Shut the fuck up Grinder. We've got work to do."

"Yeah, yeah, yeah."

"Now tell me Grinder, what happened to . . ."

"May-Li and her hostages?"

"I'm going back to 1958 Grinder, you comin'?"

“Are you crazy? Beaufort'll cut my nuts off.”

“Well where you are now you probably don't have much use for `em.”

“I'll deal with it. Thanks for meeting me CP, I always can rely—”

“You mean mooch, finagle, or scam don't you?”

“I was just sayin'.”

“Save it. I got to get back to the cornfield.”

36

May-Li RISING

I get new genes. Yes siree I got genes like fancy designer on my insides. Hahaha, now I read mind, heal like nothing, and don't age. Hahaha. May-Li have what they call "real power" and best thing is I learn how to go here, there, anywhere, and any time in.

ALL history. That make May-Li most powerful lady in world. Too bad Yankee Doodle and his lady friend from way back lost in-between place. Too-da-freaking-loo.

They never find May-Li. Now I go make some nice bank. Maybe play tomorrow stock market today to start with. Hahaha stupid Yankee Doodle.

37

BEAUFORT DOES NOT GET ANGRY

CP needed answers.

"Well, well, well CP, it seems like Nadine will be just fine—she'll rejuvenate—it may take a day maybe two but fine nonetheless. When her blood was taken it looks like some toxins—heavy metals—got slipped in. I don't quite know what that Vietnamese vixen's objective was—perhaps murder, and certainly do not know what she's hoping for with Mymine laced blood. She couldn't fathom being forever tracked, traced, and controlled by the satellites, but now? My, my, my the surprises she'll meet will most certainly be retched."

"What about Milly and that douche bag Grinder?"

"Not to worry CP, she'll be just fine." Beaufort opened a cabinet. "She's going to recover and I'm going to see if any ripples in time are disrupted."

There were several computer-like screens and objects clearly not of this era, 1958 that is. "I think it's time to do a little check up on things. Let's see what the little gal is doing with her new found, confusing, and most hazardous new 'abilities' in time and space, and put a halt to any grotesque mischief."

"Sounds like a plan Beauf." CP ran the palm of his hand down his face. "You're sure Nadine's going to be all right?"

"Not to be concerned CP, not to be concerned. She's a fine human specimen, and she'll be as fine as she ever was. Just a little tincture of time my friend, best medicine there is. For a gal from 2070 born with what you've just recently became? Consider her little brush with that mad woman."

"Murdering bitch." CP sat up straight clenched his fist and gritted his teeth."

"Think of it as a burp my friend."

“I'm gonna get that little snake Beauf, I swear it.”

“Now, now, now, all will fit into place and the mosaic of history will be restored. And yes, that scoundrel will get hers. But we MUST piece together what she's doing, with who, and why, so we can take measures so this sort of thing doesn't happen again.”

“I'm going to sit with Nadine, watch her sleep.”

“Just across the hall, go calm yourself CP, all will be well.”

38

May-Li on the Fun

After May-Li's first few trades the millions of dollars didn't appear as fashionable sitting in her 2014 online trading account. She needed to treat herself to a makeover with her swell and youthful new body.

"May-Li know lady's blood have special perks, just not so fab, and May-Li fabulous gal as can be. Now much much younger and pretty like thirty year old. Hair so nice, skin so soft. Oh May-Li going to live forever and do it in style."

Thus, May-Li went on a spending binge like any rags and nail shavings to riches person would, and when she hit the streets with a full tank of ill gotten gains, she couldn't spend as much as she made. Each day she simply bought and sold winners, and didn't consider in any form there might be consequences. “Who would think little May-Li do something not so like other people. May-Li real smart.” Having telepathic powers helped. An oceanfront townhouse, a new Bentley, and having two clerks and a security guard escort her to her car after a trip to Cartier or Tiffany's.

By all visible measures May-Li looked like someone who scored, and scored well. Her cover story was an affluent European ex-husband to be, with a very fat wallet. “Who can question that, huh Yankee Doodles?”

By happenstance the car pooped out at a stop light in Fort Lauderdale. It must have been the battery was her first thought, and it just so happened that it pooped right in front of the Squeaky Wheels high end auto repair shop. She considered a call to the dealership, with the same sort of process she decided on getting her hair done, or getting back to the mall. Which was quicker. She presented her elegant, well dressed, bejeweled self to none other than The Corporal.

“I need car fixed see—” She pointed to the pink Bentley outside. “I need it done chop chop not like Yankee Doodle always leave overnight. No no no.

You not Yankee Doodle, right? That good. Now get going, whatever it cost I have hair appointment real soon." She looked on at what a casual observer would suspect her wristwatch cost. More than a small home—on the ocean.

"We can get you right in ma'am," The Corporal said.

Across the street a man in a bespoke suit sat in a very cool and comfortable 1996 Volvo, and stared at his pocket watch.

39

EDDY FESSES UP

I don't know how I got pulled into this "thing" with Doc Beaufort—the country doc from no country anyone ever heard of—CP, Milly, Nadine, and that fucking asshole Grinder, but I did. I was "transformed" thanks to Beaufort, and given this wacky extra cyclic nucleotide that modified my genetic makeup, and yes it felt good. I stopped aging, could read minds, and be free from disease. Shit, I could live forever, but they didn't mention I could live broke, and for me, that sucked shit out of a freaking straw.

I was living as an outsider in a cabal of time traveling, space-time hopping, enforcers of history. Only I was an outsider I'd never be fully part of their little group, would I? That's what I said to myself when I moved into this bullshit condominium in Peanutville, Boca Raton in the freaking year 2014 as some sort of piker. Me, a plastic surgeon with the biggest, slickest, most envied practice in Miami in the 90s. I was king of cosmetic surgery, Lancelot of liposuction, boss of the boobs, filling A cups with whatever it took. I was the go-to-guy and the money didn't just roll in, it washed in like a damn tsunami. I had it all. All of that fell apart when the state medical board rained on my situation, and I was nixed from MD land for who knew how long. Bills mounted after the first few malpractice suits, and the unfortunate surgical candidates didn't turn out "perfect," so I accepted an invitation to meet some old classmates at some bullshit reunion.

So here I am stuck in the year 2014 living in some bullshit dump far from my estate on Key Biscayne. Sure the practice was still churning out cash, but none of it was coming my way.

Shit, I threw in with Beaufort and his crew. Some bullshit Time Enforcement Bureau which yours truly wasn't or ever would be fully part of, or privy to the secrets they had, or any control over history, life —my life—and accepted being "in" on being able to wander about through this or that era, but only at the mercy of my "handlers" which truly stunk.

I lived like a rat with no visible means or invisible way to make any bank. Occasionally I'd get a nice trip from 2014 to 1958 to hear Beaufort's long winded "Well, well, well," speeches and platitudes, but no bank. Just enjoy the life you've got.

Superpowers that few could imagine. Well, shit, I HAD superpowers as a top doc in Miami turning the twisted nose, puffy pooch, flat chested femme fatale's into beautiful creatures. That my friends was power. And that asshole Grinder and his bullshit Elvis impersonator crap reassured me how "cool" life is for people like us. Bullshit. Living on fucking cat food, and driving a beat up ten year old Mercedes wasn't living. Oh I lived fine, in fact I hadn't aged a day since I joined that troupe. I could look into a person's thoughts, and you know what? Nobody cared. The electric and phone bills were still due, the shit mortgage they arranged for a man whose identity was still twenty years after the fact "recreated" so I could fit in as a "retired" doctor living the life.

Some life. Did these Time Bureau folks pay squat for anything? No. I had to nickel and dime everything, and haggle every deal like I was a refuge from some flea market. Doc Eddy that's me, a time traveller with more time on my hands than a convict. I would've preferred just aging normally, whatever that is. But here I am a 76 year old man with the looks of a 44 year old, and fit as a twenty year old, and no fucking means of support.

Grinder popped in and out of who knew where, in his red 50s Cadillac convertible, occasionally meeting me poolside at the condo with a pep talk.

I suppose that's when it occurred to me that if I wasn't on the inside I'd have to wing it. The idea came in a flash. I'd befriended a gal at the condo, the manager, board director, or some other bullshit thing little people do when they're playing the back nine, and that's it for their lives. She was a smokin' Oriental gal named May-Li, and she was at a point where a little nip and tuck would take her 65 years and shave off thirty. I could do those things, but with no operating room, no license in the state, and a skill set from the 90s wouldn't lay a finger on her.

Maybe it was some time in mid 2014 when it hit me that I could make some bank pulling a few strings—not my strings—but the puppeteer's pulleys and tricks to pull something off.

She definitely caught Grinder's eye. He loved staring down her skimpy bikini at her double A cups rambling about what color her nipples were. Shit, Elvis, give it a break. But no, he couldn't resist some asshole commentary about Vietnam, and his heroic absence. I think he sort of fell for her, but with a guy like Grinder who never passed a mirror without combing his hair, fiddling with his mutton chops, or posing, I got the idea that maybe I could finagle my way to some way out of this place.

Grinder and I were roughly the same height and weight, and in sunglasses and the right amount of hair gel, and leather jacket I could pass for Elvis slash Grinder for a spell. All I had to do was get him to leave me his car.

40

EDDY

I first met Burt “Winner” Winn long time ago, then I met him again at the condo. He was a vendor that May-Li contracted, make that cut a deal with, to do some nonsense work to the tune of four hundred thousand dollars. Repair and replace some bullshit needs nothing done repairs for which Burt would kick back half to May-Li—sweet deal. “Winner” Winn knew how to creatively develop, or photoshop “issues” to enhance the money flow to management AKA, May-Li and her minions.

I actually “befriended” the mug when he found out I was a retired doc. How? Somehow it felt like he was instructed to check me out, see what I was all about. Who knows?

My “friend” would go out of his way, walking across the complex looking for me. I know the former doctor thing attracts cheapies—folks looking for free advice—like sugar ants to powdered sugar, but there was some inauthentic authenticity about his insincere sincerity. Sure, your pal Eddy is always up for rapping with someone especially in this zone.

The third time Burt strolled over he said, “Doc, can you take a look at something for me, huh palso?”

I'm no fan of curbside consults, but said I would. He told me he had a “funny looking thing” on his back and asked if I'd check out some skin lesions.

What the hell? I had nothing better to do with half a century worth of medical education, and from then on we were good buddies. Sort of. Never trusted the con-man, but he was an indirect stream to where the real money, or at least real enough, to get me into the good graces of the ongoing scams.

Months passed, and little by little Burt in his fulminant braggadocio couldn't help but pull me aside and tell me how easy it was to bilk a condo or homeowner's association.

I learned that Burt was some sort of property manager, and he oversaw, or I should say over charged and pocketed nearly two million dollars for misdiagnosing plumbing, electrical, elevator, or whatever problems. Then padding his invoice so fully it'd make medical insurance fraud, as in over billing, bundling fake records, and on and on. Look like an honest, by Florida standards, way to make a living. "Winner" Winn was on to something. No license, no fees, no continuing education, just a computer and a blank piece of paper to create bills for whatever he knew he could cash in on.

There were rumors he and May-Li were lovers. One look at "Winner" and his overhanging pooch, drooping jowls, and hideous skin lesions—Seborrheic dermatitis—I knew May-Li wouldn't let the guy fondle her pinky toe if her life depended on it.

Besides, his girlfriend, wife, lover, whatever, Linda seemed to keep him on a short leash. She didn't particularly care for Burt's fussing so often with May-Li. Besides she was not his type at all, and if May-Li had a type it wasn't Burt. Linda knew she was counterfeit, elegant, stylish, and pretty. Thus began the hatching of a plan.

41

CP AND NADINE

CP had been sitting in a chair next to the examination table in Beaufort's office for hours watching Nadine. Dozing off from time to time, he sat and patiently watched. Every hour or less he'd run his hand through her hair, feel her pulses, and stroke her cheek. However much time passed was irrelevant.

At this time, 1958 in Hoogerstown time was just another variable easily manipulated by Beaufort's connections. CP didn't give much of a shit as long as Nadine was going to be all right.

He saw her lids flutter, she coughed then raised her head a bit. CP was on his feet, running his hand through her hair, kissing her forehead, and then she grinned. “Kiss me you fool.”

“Shit, Nadine, my toes and lips are numb.”

“Hold me CP. Just put your arms around me and shut out the lights.”

An hour later the lights were back on, and both of them lay together, seminude on the exam table.

“You're going to be fine Nadine.” CP said, holding her tightly. “Please, don't let this happen again.”

“Now you're telling me what to do?”

“Actually I was thinking it.” He said.

“I know.” She laughed, and swung around and put both feet steadily on the Linoleum. “Good as good can be.”

“Do you remember what happened?”

“It's fuzzy. Someone, a woman took my blood, and it looked like Grinder was somehow involved in this.”

“That fucking shitbird Grinder. Always some scam.”

“It was Grinder but it wasn't Grinder. He wasn't the same Grinder we both—”

“Nadine, please don't defend that—”

“No. I got a strong sense it wasn't Grinder, and something else, there was an evil, a horrible wicked sense that left a taste in all my senses, something was awry. We're being played CP. I've got to talk to Beaufort and Milly. There's something going on.”

“What?”

She pushed him away. “Silly if I knew that I wouldn't be asking. I think we're going to have to get somewhere to make things right.”

“No, we're going home.”

“We might not have a home if what's going on IS going on. Someone's tampered with the flow of time, and that would jeopardize us all.”

“Grinder. That asshole.”

Righting themselves Nadine said, “I think we've got some work to do. How're your toes now?”

“Let's dance.” CP said.

42

DAPHNE

She's a young woman, and has an agenda. Sort of. Milly said to Nadine, so we've got to handle this delicately. Let me start the conversation, I've got a good read on her thoughts."

"Go right ahead Milly."

Daphne and the two women were in the parking lot of the complex posing as potential buyers of a condo for a grandparent. So tell me about yourself. Uh—"

"Daphne. Daphne Frellen. Pleasure to meet you." They all exchanged handshakes. "Can you, the president of the board, or the head honcho, answer some questions."

"Oh we'll get to that later, go on tell us about you." Nadine said.

"Well, my sole purpose in life is to marry a billionaire. I even wrote a children's book on it, so there." She said to Milly. I have a master's degree, and ever since I moved into my condominium became part of the board of directors, which, for your information is fabulous. And yes, the president of the facility is a woman named May-Li, and she and I are very very close."

"We have a mutual friend, that's terrific. You do know a man named Eddy? He's the plastic surgeon —retired, that is, who lives in your complex." Milly said.

"I do and he's really something . . . I just don't know what that something is."

Nadine chimed in, "I'm great friends with him, and look at his work." She stood up and did a full veronica showing off her figure, and then touched her fingers to her face. He's a real miracle worker."

"Was, Nadine. Years ago he had the top practice in Miami." Milly said.

“Oh, that's right. But he's a terrific guy. Have you seen him lately?” Nadine asked.

Daphne shook her head. “He's a sort of a shut-in, a hermit or something like that. Very strange guy.”

“Who isn't sweetheart?” Milly added. “Who isn't?”

43

CHECK THE SCORE IN 2014

Milly and Nadine traveled to 2014—That's where Doc Beaufort discovered the quiver in the space-time continuum. Nadine befriended Daphne accidentally on purpose at the condominium where Eddy was sent. Actually sentenced because Beaufort's sense about Eddy was less than comfortable, and despite Eddy's misgivings, Beaufort suggested Eddy could be sent quite simply to the Middle East, Africa, or some icy town way north of Lake Erie.

"Well, well, well, Eddy's too self-serving a man to lose his tan, or put himself in harms way. He'll do as we say. He knows."

At the time after Nadine's awakening Beaufort said: “Not to be concerned, Edward is much accustomed to being what he is now. He'll accommodate or—”

“I don't think we'll stroll through the cornfield,” CP said.

“Don't be silly CP, all you need is this,” Beaufort held up his the fourth finger of his left hand. He pointed it less than a foot away and a distortion of the space began. It started as a small blurry hole that enlarged gradually until a shimmering door of warped light laid over whatever reality they were in. It looked like a circus mirror, a rippling of the room's space opened. “That easy CP.”

“Damn that looks like a wedding band finger wormhole.”

“Well, well, well, many folks view marriage as trip through time and space. Why not use the right finger?”

“How did you do that?”

“Things have evolved and time travel can be accomplished via a focus of subatomic energy, and the satellites from 2090. Yes there've been some innovations since your first brush with time travel in the cornfield. The Time Bureau has gotten much more sophisticated. Think of it as an iPhone 9000—technology moves on and on, always developing."

"Am I going?" CP asked.

"Well, well, well, CP you've gathered so much hostility for Grinder and Eddy perhaps you should remain here and take care of patients. I'm going on a little trip myself."

"What?"

"I need to visit a certain auto repair shop, and check in on the shenanigans May-Li's been up to. Apparent ripples in time began after she purchased a pink Bentley and connected with some less than stellar specimens."

"Ladies, are you ready to pay Eddy a visit?" Doc Beaufort said just before to sending them to the year 2014.

"He's going to have a fit." CP said.

"He earned it." Milly said.

"He sure did." Nadine walked over to CP and kissed him. "We'll be fine. Just lunch with the girls."

44

EDDY AWAKES TO THE SOUND OF BIRDS

Eddy awoke on the side of the road. He didn't know which road, but it sure's shootin' wasn't any road he'd ever seen. He'd lain there groggily staring at the cloudless predawn sky until a flock of birds began hovering overhead. “A gaggle of geese?” He said out loud until that gaggle started increasing bird-wise, and realized those weren't geese they were vultures. Shit. He brought himself to his feet and looked around. He was in a desert, some isolated place in what could have been Nevada, Utah, or some other flyover state. Mountains in the distance, and no sign of life other than critters and cactus as far as he could see. And what year is this? The road looked like it hand't been paved in half a century or more. Shit lost in time, and for what?

His mouth was dry, and he needed a sip of something, anything, but in this desolate place there was nothing. No cars, trucks, or any sign of human life as far as he could see. Nada.

He patted his pockets—a leather jacket? There was a pack of cigarettes, sunglasses, and a comb. Shit, he was still dressed as the man he impersonated—Grinder. The Ostrich boots made his toes numb, and the hair gel felt sticky and it stunk. He ran his hand along his scalp, no bugs or lizards, and felt the mutton chop sideburns.

How did I get here was among the first thoughts. Followed by how the hell he'd get out of this place. The hills looked a thousand miles away, the sand had no occasional tufts of cacti, nada. He'd have to hoof it—maybe find something or someone and hitch a ride into whatever middle of nowhere place he could get to. He couldn't get the gears of his consciousness to budge, and with each try a thought squeaked out like an oilless engine. Damn, he looked up at the hovering scavenger birds, and flipped the universal "fuck you" sign. "I may be a wreck but ain't no way I'm ready to be bird food."

Shit, shit, shit on a stick. He began walking with the sort of intent a man headed for the gallows—in his mind—might think or feel. Oddly Eddy didn't feel much, other than a thick slice of knowledge that he'd truly screwed things up.

Who sent me here? He asked himself. Who, who, who? When it occurred to him the country doc from 1958 and his little deal with the Oriental gal, May-Li. Was this punishment, abandonment, or some kind of retribution for getting a job done? Shit, Eddy thought, he had to make a living. Why me? He walked on and the sun rose higher in the sky. It was going to get much hotter, he removed the jacket and draped it over his shoulder. Onward we go, he said to himself. And he marched along like a good soldier reminding himself that he'd seriously made poor choices. This was a biggy. Will I ever get out of this place?

EDDY'S MIND WANDERS

Eddy'd been walking for hours. He could feel the sun's heat beat down on him, and knew he'd be toasty, dehydrated, and all kinds of screwed up in another hour or so. He took off his shirt and wrapped it around his head like some bedouin trekking toward an oasis, but there was nothing but mirage after mirage, and his mind began playing memories, speeches, periodic tables, Krebs' Cycle, and anything that stuck just to stay alert, or as aware as possible. Shit, there were all sorts of screwy critters out here.

He flashed memory of a wedding he was invited to but never showed up for, and replayed the speech he would've given. Damn, the hallucinations are kicking in. Damn, damn, damn. He read his regret for not attending letter out loud and to the birds, the stinking birds dammit. It went like this:

MEMORIES OR SOME CORNY BULL FROM THE DAMNNED IMPLANTS

A remarkable trajectory of life's winding, winsome, wildly, weird wonders. Events occur as markers on this plane, often unexpected delights, sometimes fraught with fright, yet always consistent in the flow of the currents of our lives.

You can't step in the same river twice, or so they say. So when you plunge into this thing from the womb on what's least expected becomes one among many jolts to what is, what was, and what will be.

New beginnings and promise of things to come ignite a glimpse of the majesty of the marvels without any foreshadowing.

There'll always be some tributary, a splintered flow in time's currents, but nothing brings more joy than watching a new beginning, and the road unvisited.

So there it is, this thing—life, and all it brings whether grief, pleasure, strife, or an unexpected gift at an unexpected time along that line from cradle on, and all we can do is reflect upon those simple moments when wishes become realized.

We wish you great joy in the knowledge that all's well, and the wind remains in your sail. Enjoy the best times, forget the worst, store them away for a crummy day—and rejoice in what's become.

Eddy stopped walking, and stood there with his hands on his hips. "What the fuck I'm starting to think like a chick?"

He slapped himself twice—hard, and took out one of Grinder's cigarettes. "Shit I gotta get it together or I'll be singing love songs to those fucking vultures." He lit up a smoke, coughed, and let the nicotine do its job.

"Stay snapped out of it Eddy," he coughed again and felt a burst of chemicals pass his blood brain barrier.

Talking to himself, stumbling, holding his hand up to the salute an unforgiving sky.

"This sucks but it beats getting all sappy. I wish I was back at my place, jump in the pool and stay there for a month."

He walked on, flipping the bird to the birds.

I'm losin' it, man, Eddy thought with each long lugubrious, painful step. I'm fucking losing it. Shit, Eddy thought, he'd never wax nostalgic, but this?

Did those guys–Beaufort and crew–implant some emote juju in me? Am I becoming more chick than dude–Ask a vulture, right? But I'm "fixed" I rejuvenate, so I can't get that fucked up, right? Keep telling myself that, and all this will be reversed as soon as I . . . I what? Where am I going? Maybe that bitch May-Li did this, that little ho. Shouldn't have agreed to help her, shouldn't have gotten too hungry, or shone it—to anyone, anywhere, any how. No. I fucked up. I got greedy and couldn't just play it as it lays. That's what CP would say, no mulligan, you land in a sand trap you deal with it, and I didn't. So this is my penance—please let this be that. It can't get much worse, or can it?

The birds were hovering closer to the walking man, and as the sun hit its zenith he had to sit. Had to find some shade behind a cactus or some other desert flower—FLOWER? Shit, he thought, there's no freaking flowers in the desert in . . . Could they have sent me off in some space-time convoluted ripple off to some zone on the planet where people carried AK-47s? Damn, CP wouldn't do that to me, he owes me. Right, he OWES me, or does he? Could have really fucked up. Got to keep walking.

Two hours and forty two minutes later a plume of dust kicked up in the distance. Eddy saw it and moved as far from the road, and behind the thickest desert weeds he could find. He heard an engine hum. A truck of some kind, slow, steady, and heading this way.

He covered himself with the leather jacket, and watched, waited, and listened as whatever was approaching grew near. Could it be a military thing, some rebel army out for heads to hunt? Guns, killers, shit, can't rejuvenate from a full kill, or can you? Don't want to find out now do I? Eddy watched as the plume grew into a mushroom cloud, and the sound of its engine got louder. It sounded like some old truck or junker making its way across the sea of sand. Should I flag it down?

It was a red pickup truck. He could see it approach lumbering along like it made this road its own. From maybe a half mile away he saw the driver: a man in a cowboy hat, could've been a chick, but at a quarter mile Eddy'd swear he'd never seen a chick so homely. This was some sort of desert rat hillbilly. Who, why, what? Shit who cares, I'm gonna flag it down, he said to himself. Eddy gathered himself and walked quickly to the side of the road and waited.

It seemed like a lifetime until the red pickup creaked, sputtered, and was a hundred yards or less away. Eddy stuck both arms up and waved. He swung the jacket around like a distress signal, and heard the vehicle's brakes squeak, and finally come to a stop.

Eddy had nothing to lose, and pensively walked toward the driver's side door. A filthy ancient piece of shit truck. As he approached the trucks's window came down and the driver, cowboy hat, sunglasses, and a Mossberg made that undeniably unique sound of a shell being racked into place.

“Howdy doody stranger,” the driver said. “You ain't some terrorist or somethin' are you?”

“Shit no. I'm a doctor”.

“Well hellfire boy I'm your ride.”

“Who're you?”

“The name's Eustice. Eustice Seeney, and Doc Beaufort sent me on out to give you lift. That is if your name's Eddy, is it?”

“I'm Eddy.”

“Well then collsarn it, get in and have something to drink, got plenty, and enjoy the ride.”

“Where are you taking me?”

“I don't know for sure, but the Doc says to just pick you up and lend a hand. You comin'?”

Eddy narrowed his eyes expecting who knew what. One glance at the sun and he said: “Sure, what've I got to lose?”

“Ain't got nothin' to lose buddy, the Doc don't do crummy stuff so you can be sure you're in good hands.”

“Eustice?”

“That's me boy, what're you waitin' for? I'm gettin' a sunburn just sittin' here and the engine's gettin' hot. Hop in Eddy.”

45

HOW TO ARGUE WITH YOUR SPOUSE

CP was left alone in the office while Beaufort was off doing his thing. The girls were off somewhere else. Dammit. He asked her to stay but no, Nadine insisted. He practically begged her not to go. Milly went off to some era that could be truly hazardous, maybe even kill her, shit. As Beaufort explained to him before he left, “CP you've got to learn to accept without accepting. Everything will be just fine.”

“Blah, blah, wise advice,” CP had said moments before he transported himself. “Trust me, CP, I've been with Milly for nearly four hundred years. Some things aren't worth quarreling over. You've got to know when to let things go.”

"How long? Shit, that's—" CP was counting on his fingers. "Forty decades?"

"Quite some time CP, quite some time. You'll learn. You'll learn."

"What about arguing?" CP asked, as Beaufort slipped into some clothing fitting the era he was going to.

"I think when you're in a relationship—say a marriage, a long one, a couple discovers how to 'argue' successfully." Beaufort said.

"How do you fight with someone successfully?"

"Well, well, well, after a decade or so you already learn what buttons to push to agitate, irritate, aggravate, and drive someone nuts."

"And what?"

"And you use those same skills, knowing what 'buttons' to be mindful of, what's worth quarreling over, and what's just silly. Most tit for tat nonsense between a man and woman—not so politically correct—are based on nonsense. You mature into understanding each other's style of arguing, their hot-button topics, and you learn after some time what to avoid. Understanding, and being kind when you're simmering."

"And that works for you, eh?"

"That's been the template I've found most conducive to a harmonious relationship."

"Shit" CP said, and turned to thank Doc Beaufort. He was already gone.

46

MAY-LI IN MIAMI

The penthouse suite of the high-rise was among the worlds most exclusive addresses. May-Li could look out over the world and say: “I win Yankee Doodle, I win!”

She often did this before going to sleep, in the wee hours, or upon awakening after one of many beauty naps thanks to the modified DNA she “borrowed” from Nadine with help from Eddy. She considered tossing him a gift, but no . . . that fool work for May-Li.

Thusly that Thursday afternoon after her brief swim, walk on the beach, and settling onto her sofa to watch TV she fell asleep. One hour and sixteen minutes later she awoke to what she considered some horrible show and started clicking away.

"Click, click, click. Why channel no change? What is this shit? I call maintenance, click, click. Holy Toledo, what is this?" She held up her hand and saw her nails had broken off with each click.

She saw the flesh of her hand in the late afternoon sun; wrinkled, veiny, and bony as Kentucky Fried wings, that had been eaten by some pigs. She dashed off to her well appointed master bathroom and saw her face in the mirror. "What's this?"

She ran a hand through her long, and formerly dark hair May-Li's hair turned white? What is this shitty shit shit. She fussed with it tugging disgustedly, and it came out in clumps. Her legs began shaking, and she looked at her teeth, they'd rotted. From out of nowhere she heard whomp whomp whomp. "Holy shit what's that? Sound like Vietnam."

She looked outside at what should have been Miami's best and saw nothing but filthy run down housing, ancient vehicles on the road, and rickshaws. "Rickshaws! What is this—" She heard explosions in the distance, jets flying overhead, and ran inside. “Where am I?”

She reached for the TV clicker and nothing was on. The magazines she had cluttered about weren't in English, they were in her native language. “Shit, shit, shit I kill whoever do this to May-Li,” but she couldn't budge.

Something overtook her and her face went numb, fingers without sensation, and her vision blurred. She tried to find the phone, and realized she'd become old, very old, and very weak in a world far away from the fantasy she thought she'd stolen.

47

BEAUFORT GOES TO THE AUTO REPAIR SHOP IN 2014

The driver of the 1996 Volvo walked into the Squeaky Wheels repair shop and asked for whoever was in charge. He said he was having some car trouble. "The Corporal" looked at the well dressed, soft spoken man the way a clerk at Saks looks at a stumble bum—ready to call security. Being who he was, "The Corporal" couldn't resist calling his cousin Chip, to see this piece of work, and remind him that he and the ancient Volvo were way below the stature of someone who'd have much use for their facility.

Chip had a rag in his hands which he used to rub whatever filth may have gotten on him. After all, Chip had a date later that night with Daphne, and a loser like this guy? Shit, he winked at his cousin in that, "maybe we can take him for a few bucks" look. He cleared his throat, almost chuckling and spoke in a snotty, trenchant, tone: "How can we help you and your Volvo?"

At that, Doc Beaufort reached into his suit coat, removed two sets of documents and thrust them at Chip and his cousin. "Boys you've just been drafted."

"Are you nuts you freak?"

The room began to spin and the lights flickered. There was a burst of thunder and the showroom went berserk: cars revved, items fell off shelves, and a pane of glass broke. Something about the atmosphere changed, and a gust of icy air made the cousins shiver.

"Who the fuck are you?"

Beaufort pointed his finger at Chip, then his cousin. At that moment a lighting bolt catapulted across the sky followed by another, and another, and both men were gone.

"Poof boys. You both looked like a change of scene would suit you just fine." Beaufort walked into the garage passing the sign that said: "Employees

Only" and stared at the pink Bentley. "Well, well, well, we're going to have some curious times with this." He inspected the vehicle, just as one of the mechanics, a man of Hispanic descent, approached. "I want you to saw this car in half," Beaufort said removing a roll of bills.

"You crazy man? This is a fine automobile."

"It's not yours is it? You can check with your bosses, but I believe they're somewhat indisposed. One hundred thousand dollars US?"

The mechanic stared at him.

Beaufort read his thoughts, maybe another fifty thousand? "Cash young man, right here right now."

"Thass sounding good man."

"One more thing before you start." Beaufort said.

The mechanic was fondling the money. "Anything you want boss."

"I want you to call Chip's girl, and tell her to meet him at this address." Beaufort handed him a slip of paper. "Here's another ten thousand."

At that, the mechanic went to town on that pink car.

48

A RIGHTFUL PLACE IN THE SCHEME OF THINGS

History layers over itself, folding over and over again. So the world you experience is a version—the most perfect that is—to ensure a certain balance on the planet. You see, certain things are meant to occur and occasionally folks slip through the cracks and live out their lives. When in fact according to the "most walkable tightrope theory" the founders of the Time Bureau constructed several models whereby a certain balance was to be maintained. Certainly wars, epidemics, atrocities, and so much more man has done or been party to. Calculated out millions and millions of times, the best possible outcomes were found to ensure life on earth remained habitable for the larger parts of humanity. We're not talking about catching rotten disease before it spreads, assassinating a Hitler, or stopping the cellphone wars, we're talking about sustainable life on earth. Many things involving millions and millions happen, but they're meant to happen. Tyrannies arise and horrible things happen, not so much as some cosmic trick rather a maintenance of balance on the planet.

“There's only enough water and food on this planet.” Beaufort said.

“You're talking population control, euthanasia, letting the most powerful armies encircle the earth. Is that what you're saying?”

“In some ways it's the natural order of things, and as many variations. Some stretching out to the infinite became possible to calculate some time. far, far, off in a future beyond any could imagine. The earth needed the best possible chance to survive.”

“Are you saying there's been this cabal of 'masters' who've engineered our lives, all of our lives?”

“Unfortunately or perhaps fortunately there was no 'secret society' or conspiracy. There were calculations, meteors that could have destroyed it all. Maintaining the balance was a mathematical exercise that evolved. In many ways technology evolved like our own brutal human savagery. Sadly for man some people were not meant to survive that storm, war, or disease."

"You're saying it's your job to maintain something a thousand years in the future so we don't screw it up?"

"Let me make it simple CP. Eddy, who became what he did, impacted many lives. The sad metrics are that Eddy and May-Li were never meant to live beyond the early 1970s. They jiggled their own destinies."

"What?"

"In 1970 Eddy was drafted and would have died in a rice paddy, May-Li would have been killed in a tunnel. Those trajectories ARE how things were meant to be. Eddy became a 'conscientious objector' and avoided that war. May-Li was taking care of the nails of the tunnelers, and by a ragged cuticle a digger died in her place."

"So Eddy went on to do what he did, considering how many patients he accidentally' killed?"

“How many?”

“There were two failed diagnosis of clotting disorders, and the emboli lodged in their hearts. What would they have become? Would a great distiller of water, an inventor of a solar flare detector have been born? Would that fellow with a bad nail have gone on to find a way to remove nuclear weapons from the always at war populous?”

“I don't know.” CP said.

“The supercomputers thousands of years hence knew, and men and women like Milly and me, Nadine, you too, even Grinder are part of making this world as good of a place as it can be.”

“Shit Beauf, I didn't think of it like that.”

“It's a tough pill to swallow.”

“I've taken a few, and I guess what needs to be done we do.” CP said. “By the way, what exactly was Grinder's deal?”

Beaufort held up his hand, and shook his head. “Well, well, well CP, we'll get around to it.”

49

BACK TO 1970

The hotel had seen better days. Probably when Vietnam was home to the French, who built extravagant eateries, bars, and hotels. Saigon was in some folks minds to be a sort of miniature Paris.

However, the war seemed to take the Paris Hilton of Saigon more toward some rickety, smoke filled, loud, drinking hole for soldiers, mercenaries, and spies. The Bamboo chairs were frazzled replacements for the leather seats, and the tables all of them, shimmied and shook with each blast of overflying choppers and jets. The beaded curtains took the place of doors, and the once elegant Mahogany bar was splintered and pocked with cigarette holes, grime, and a lingering scent of cordite hung heavy in the air wafting about via the slow turning ceiling fans. Paris Hilton wouldn't find the place in 1970 quite so chi chi. Then again she wouldn't have been born.

Among the hotel bars patrons was an odd couple. A very young woman dressed for dinner and dancing in an evening gown, bedecked in jewelry. One of the men at the bar—a soldier would later recall to his platoon he saw someone who just walked off the set of the Great Gatsby. His Lieutenant dismissed it as an hallucination.

Oh yeah, there were two other soldiers at the bar. Enlisted men sipping slow beers, smoking, talking in hushed tones, and not seeming to give a crap about anything, probably planning to go AWOL. One of them looked old enough to be someone's grandfather, the other a real weaselly looking guy, jumpy as hell. Neither checked out the babe.

"That place is filled with all sorts of crumbs," the Lieutenant said.

"I heard the broad's name, the waiter called her Daphne." It seemed like he knew her. The soldier from the bar said she was gorgeous, but the old man she was with looked like he might have keeled over if she leaned and showed some cleavage. Which the soldier said was unlikely because she appeared to be hating life. “Oh well Corporal, that's what you get when you're vacationing in a war zone.”

“I think the guy was that Nigel something or other, the billionaire ex-pat.”

“You're saying you saw the infamous Nigel? No way soldier, that guy never leaves his yacht.”

“I heard he married some young chippy,” another man cleaning his weapon chimed in.

“That's right soldier, young dame snags a codger and lives the life. Aah, to be back in the world.” The Lieutenant said wistfully.

“Oh yeah LT, the strangest shit happened. I was walking out of the joint and some whacked out old Vietnamese broad was yelling at the bartender about her Bentley being messed with. She looked like death on a cracker. Man did she make a scene.”

“She could've been NVA.” The lieutenant said.

“I had to split, but on my way out the brass was on the way in. A full bird Colonel and two Majors. They had a black Sergeant with them—big guy, one of the Majors had him guard the door. Shit I was going to salute, but it looked like some serious shit was going down"

"A full bird Colonel?" The Lieutenant said.

What's that? One of the recruits in the platoon thought. He looked over at the other Private, a man who once had the title "The Corporal" and looked at the soldier next to him. A man whose name patch said "Chip" across his right breast pocket.

Neither of these men had ever been in uniform, and couldn't make squat out of how to ready their weapons. Both would be missing in action by week's end.

The man named Chip looked at the former Corporal, his cousin, and said "Daphne?"

"You didn't salute and a full bird and two Majors didn't pull your chain?"

"Nope. I think they were still chuckling about the pink Bentley out front that'd been sawed in half and made into a rickshaw, and getting things set up for who knows what. I just wanted my ass out of there."

50

CHECKING IN BEFORE CHECKING OUT

The two men who remained in the bar didn't see the Colonel or two Majors walk in. The three officers stood directly behind them and waited a beat before the Colonel cleared his throat.

Both uniformed beer drinkers, both Privates, one notably older and drawn, the other much younger, turned their heads at the same time to see the full bird Colonel, and stood up, finally giving feeble salutes.

“Well, well, well boys, or should I say gentlemen shouldn't I? Burt and Eddy. You two far from your unit?”

The two men studied the three officers reading their name patches: Colonel Beaufort, Majors CP, and Grinder, and sat back down. The older man took a sip of his beer. “We don't have a stinking 'unit' we just—”

“Appeared, didn't you?” Major Grinder said.

“Yeah, that's what happened. I don't belong here, I'm a CO.” Eddy whose recollection of things that haven't happened was fuzzy.

“Future history works that way. You have shadows of what could have been, but nothing tangible or fixed.” Beaufort said.

“What do you guys want?” Eddy said.

“That's no way to talk to an officer.” Major CP said.

“You guys are spooks, and there's no way you're recruiting me. I can speak for my young friend here, he was going to be a doctor.” Burt said.

“So I've heard,” Colonel Beaufort said.

“Why ARE you here?” Eddy said.

“Well, well, well, it's important to see that everything finds its place, and every place has its things. You two fellows are right where you belong. By the way, in another life that white haired woman with car trouble and you fellows could have done very well together if—”

“What'd I ever do, kill someone in a past life?” Eddy said. “That's bull.” Eddy grabbed his drink and chugged it.”

“Well, yes fellows you may very well have, but maybe it wasn't a past life, just another plane of this one.” The Colonel said.

“Total bullshit.” Eddy belched. “I never did nothin'.”

“Nah, Eddy. You never pretended to be someone that looked like me, did you?” Major Grinder said.

Eddy seemed shaken as if someone invaded a dream and stirred him from sleep. “No way, I ain't done nothin'.”

“Something happened in a parking lot of a strip mall, and both of you mugs or some iteration of yourselves were there." Major CP said. "I can't expect you to understand."

Colonel Beaufort would later explain how remnants of memories, things yet to be created, incomplete neural pathways "like a cloth that's been washed too often reverse, fade, and the fabric of reality is an incomplete tattered and confusing blanket of brain cells."

"This is bullshit. I never did nothing wrong." Eddy folded his arms across his chest. "Nothing."

"Me neither Colonel. I've got a woman back home, I think I still do, don't I?" Burt said.

"Linda's just where she belongs, and she'll be just fine." Colonel Beaufort said. "However you two were really never meant to be. She did something quite rotten, and there is no statute of limitations on that sort of thing. She may be relocated to one of the state's finer penal institutions. Her former husband Lem, died of a gunshot wound to the leg, it hit the femoral artery and he bled out. He was on Coumadin. The gash to the head was unnecessary, just the brutal act of a bully."

“What?” The older soldier said, his eyes glazed over. “Hey palso.” Immediately Burt “Winner” Winn regretted mouthing off to an officer. “I mean sir,” he said to Colonel Beaufort. “The guy was on blood thinners? Shit.” Followed by saying minga dinga minga dinga to himself four or five times.

“Well, well, well, Private Winn, I am not your palso. A man your age should know how to address a superior officer.” Beaufort shook his head examining the buffoon in uniform. A Buck Private old enough to have been retired. Beaufort marveled at Winn's accelerated aging. There were wrinkles, and skin creases with more hideous lesions then he could count.

Burt “Winner” Winn had no Mymine implants to neutralize, the way Eddys were. Beaufort would later tell CP and Grinder. “His thoughts would remain more intact.”

“That's friggin' bull, Winn.” Major Grinder said.

“I didn't have anything to do with that. Burt “Winner” Winn I was just following orders. Why punish me?”

“But you didn't merely follow orders. You made up your own, and now you're right where you belong.” Colonel Beaufort said.

“At ease men. Have another beer on me.” Major Grinder tossed a twenty on the counter. “We've got to get going, so carry on.”

“Carry on? Hang on a second, we belong somewhere else, don't we?” Eddy said.

“No. You're just where you should be. Always were, and always will be.” Major CP added.

“We're going to be leaving now.” Beaufort said.

“I suppose so.” CP added.

“That was an example of the explosion of memory. A test of sorts of the system.”

“What system?” Major Grinder said as they stood at the front door.”

“Shut up, Grinder.” CP said. “What kind of test?”

“A test we passed, and balance we can be assured is restored.”

“What'm I missing here?” Grinder pushed on the door.

“Given a visual trigger, a memory cue results in a cascade of recollections, and some things snap into a crystallization in the consciousness of those who've been replanted in time.” Beaufort said.

“Time is the great constant, a reminder of things gone and lost for good.” CP said.

“We just witnessed remnants of time travel memory. The cascade of memories—even those lost or forgotten—brings them into focus if only briefly with the proper evocation.” Beaufort said. “Thus, memory chains do not remain in their entirety without a conductor to tap the baton.”

“Those guys were busted like a ripe zit,” Grinder said holding the door open for CP and Beaufort.

“Grinder, I rarely make a disparaging comment, but shut the fuck up.” Doc Beaufort said.

Grinder looked at the black man guarding the door. “I don't think we gotta worry about those douche whistles going anywhere Chalk.”

"You had me suit up in my old uniform, go out to a cornfield to watch the door Grinder? Shish, man—not cool."

"Mr. Chalk we needed you and you delivered, for that I am grateful you passed the first test." Colonel Beaufort said.

"Test? Nobody said nothin' about no test." Chalk said.

"Welcome to the Time Bureau," CP said.

"Well, well, well, gentlemen I think it wise we get going." Beaufort said.

The four of them walked out the door, and the three officers boarded the rickshaw Bentley. Chalk was at the helm.

"Chalk, remember my asking you about swiping half a car?"

"You still crazy CP." Chalk said maneuvering the curios cut apart vehicle. "Of course I remember. Chalk don't forget nothin'. And I also remember I got some interest accruing at the favor bank. Where to officers?"

"Yes you do my man," Grinder said.

"I ain't your man honky." Chalk said.

"This isn't the 70s Chalk." Grinder said.

"Shut the hell up Grinder. It IS the 1970s." CP reminded him.

"Yeah asshole." Chalk added.

"Just get us across the street," CP said. "We owe you Chalk, just one more thing."

"Well, well, well, I think we best bust the proverbial move. I verily believe we've dissolved a most unwholesome clot in a leg of the space-time continuum." Colonel Beaufort was looking at his pocket watch."

"I'm ready to get outta this friggin' place." Grinder said.

"Yeah, I got some bidnet." Chalk said.

The colonel held up the fourth finger of his left hand, looked around, and finally pointed it. At that, a shimmering curtain of quivering light appeared. A distortion in the fabric of this 1970 reality.

“Gentlemen it's time for us to leave this place.” Beaufort stepped into the portal followed by CP, Grinder, and Chalk. “We'll drop this vehicle off along the way, and return things to their proper order. Thanks to Chalk.”

“Thass right. I got my homeboy Ramone ready to put that Bentley all right well. CP said I'd be gettin' a call, and I got it covered. Ramone can put together a ride as fast as he can take it apart. We cool?”

“Thank you Chalk, that's the plan.” CP said. “I knew you'd do it.”

“You got that right. Chalk say he gonna deliver, he deliver. Dig?”

At that they disappeared into the space-time continuum.

An onlooker riding a bicycle would recall three Yankee officers and a black Sergeant in a pink Bentley rickshaw. He watched them vanish into what looked like a huge rippling mirror that shut with a barely audible pop. This memory would remain with him for years. He liked to think it was that moment when he decided to someday study quantum physics at Stanford after this mess was over.

Just as the last man's foot entered the portal it closed. One minute and fourteen seconds after, the four men were away from the building. It suffered a devastating blow. The history books reflect the hotel's destruction to a stray bomb from an off course fighter jet.

There were no reported casualties.

www.ingramcontent.com/pod-product-compliance
Lightning Source LLC
Chambersburg PA
CBHW032117170626
46808CB00006B/1974

9780692314685